Rhapsody of the Sea

Sons of Poseidon
Book 1

Diana Long

To my husband who believed in me enough to push me into the deep end and tell me I could swim.

Note to reader

This book is intended for mature audiences. It contains adult matter such as:

- Explicit sex scenes
- Sexual assault (not caused by any of the main characters)
- Mention of rape (not caused by any of the main characters)

Chapter 1

Lyss

"Can you believe how big it is?"

"That's what she said."

My best friend, Gia, rolled her eyes at our roommate, Julie, while Clara and I snickered behind them. Our Uber had just dropped us off at the house owned by *Sons of Poseidon*, one of the hottest bands to emerge in the past couple of years. We had no idea what the parking situation would be like when we left, but seeing it now, we were glad we didn't drive. It would have been a pain in the ass to park two blocks away, if not more.

I linked my arm through Gia's and kept us walking forward. "Yes, Gia, it's huge. What do you expect from freaking rock stars?"

"I can't believe we got an invite to a *Sons of Poseidon* party," Clara squealed.

"You didn't get an invitation, Gia did," I reminded her. Gia gave my arm a quick squeeze.

"The invite said I could bring a friend or two, so you guys are as invited as I am," she said.

"Who knew call-in radio competitions were real and not just a scam to get people's hopes up," Julie said.

"Gia did," I sang.

We stood at the end of a short line to get in. A burly man with black pants and a tight black t-shirt with "security" written across the chest stood at the bottom of the steps to the front door.

"Invite," he demanded with a bored expression.

Gia showed him her phone with the invite on it.

He stared at the screen before saying, "It says a friend or two. You have three."

Gia's smile fell. "I didn't think it was literal. I thought it meant I couldn't bring a bunch of people. I only brought three."

He shrugged. "Sorry, it says it right there. I don't make the rules."

"Come on, you can make an exception, can't you?" Clara smiled and twirled her hair. She literally twirled a section of hair around her finger. I groaned inwardly with second-hand embarrassment.

"I'll just head home," I said before things got any more awkward.

"Lyss, you can't leave me here alone," Gia protested.

"You have Julie and Clara," I said.

Gia arched a perfectly shaped brow at me. My bestie was a cosmetologist, and she looked the part every second of the day. Even when she first woke up in the morning with no makeup and bed hair, she looked like a model.

"Can I have you ladies move to the side while you figure this out?" The security guy asked.

I looked behind us at the line that was forming, and we moved over to finish our discussion.

"You guys are the big fans. I like the music, but I'll be okay if I don't get into the party," I said.

"It's my mistake, I should be the one to go home," Gia said.

I started laughing. She was the biggest fan of all, especially when it came to the drummer. There was no way I was letting her leave.

"You're the one who won the tickets. You can't go home," Julie said. "Why don't we do paper, rock, scissors or something?"

"Guys, I'm fine with going home. I have work I can do, and I just got a new—"

"Book," the three of them said together.

I crossed my arms. "Well, I did. And I worked the morning shift at the diner today."

"Come on, Lyss. You can't hide in a book all the time," Gia said.

"I don't do it all the time." My lips pursed as I attempted to defend myself. I couldn't deny that I'd rather curl with a good book most of the time though.

"Right, and Clara doesn't bring a new guy home every weekend." Julie nudged Clara with her elbow.

"I don't," Clara said. "Sometimes it's the same guy two weekends in a row."

We all laughed because Gia and Julie were right about both Clara and I, even if they dramatized it a bit much.

"Now that it's settled, I'm going to head home." I pulled out my phone to order an Uber.

"Nothing has been decided," Gia said. "Put your phone away so we can figure this out."

"Is there a problem?" A shirtless, blond man with swim trunks hanging low on his hips asked as he came up to us.

"No, we're fine." I turned to close off our small group, hoping to give the very firm hint we didn't need help from some random Adonis.

Gia's eyes were wide and her mouth was open on a silent gasp as she stared at me in distress.

"What?" I asked.

"That's Ledger St. James," she hissed.

Oops. Drummer of the band, party boy, and man whore, according to Clara. And Gia's biggest celebrity crush. The girls had given me a rundown on the band before we came so I wouldn't look like a complete idiot. Guess not all of it stuck.

"Our invitation said the winner could only bring one or two friends." Julie took it on herself to explain our situation to the rock star I just snubbed. "We didn't think it meant it literally, so we're one person over and trying to decide who has to bail."

"I can help with that." Ledger's grin widened. "You can all be my personal guests for the night."

"It's fine, really." I fought the urge to roll my eyes. My new book was looking better by the minute. "I'm going to head home. There's no point in making a big deal about this."

"You don't want to come to my tour wrap up party?" Ledger asked, sounding more surprised than upset.

I shrugged. "I just know my friends want to be here more."

Ledger nodded. "Well, I get final say on the guest list, and I'm sure you'd all rather be here together."

"Yes, we would." Guess Gia finally found her voice.

"Then it's settled. You're all my personal guests. No strings attached." He aimed the last part at me.

Gia grabbed my arm and gave me a look that said, *pretty, pretty please agree to this, and if you don't, I'll shave your head while you sleep.*

"Thanks, this is really sweet of you," I said to Ledger through gritted teeth.

"Sweet is what I do." He winked at Gia, and I thought she was going to melt into the ground.

The security guard narrowed his eyes at us as we walked past the front of the line and up the steps to the front door. I shrugged my shoulders and smiled brightly at him.

"Any of you want a drink?" Ledger asked once we were inside.

We all nodded and followed him through the house. Girls in bikinis walked around holding red solo cups. Guys flaunted their abs and flexed their biceps, mentally comparing their dick sizes. I felt overdressed in cutoff jean shorts and a crop top. The invite had mentioned a pool, but I didn't know the dress code would be so little.

A bar was set up in the backyard, complete with a bartender. I grabbed a bottled water from the cooler filled with ice next to the bar and stood to the side while the girls ordered their favorite mixed drinks.

"Just water, huh?" Ledger asked.

"I have no memory of my twenty-first birthday. I remember the day after, though. It involved loads of puking and the worst headache ever." I unscrewed the cap and took a swallow of the cold water. "Ever since then, it's been water only. Soda if I'm feeling feisty."

Ledger's ever-present grin widened, showing off his dimples. Why were dimples so hot on a guy? I saw why Gia was obsessed with the playboy. He moved onto Julie and I was released from his spell.

I let Gia know I was heading out back to find us a spot and went to scope out the area. People splashed in the large pool, others lounged on the chaises next to it. One couple was going at it pretty hard against a palm tree. Her hand was between their bodies and I could only guess at what she was grabbing. I settled on an empty lounge chair and people-watched.

A guy walked towards me and I pretended to ignore him so he didn't start talking to me. I shot him an annoyed glare when he stopped next to me.

"Sorry, but do you mind if I grab my towel?" He pointed to the ground.

I looked down and saw a towel with a phone sitting under the lounge I was on.

Guilt at treating him like some creep colored my cheeks.

"Oh, I didn't realize the seat was taken." I stood up and gestured to the lounge chair. "I'll go find somewhere else to chill."

"You're fine. I just needed to grab these." He reached under the lounge and pulled out his towel and phone. "Sit back down. I'll leave. There are plenty of chairs around."

His sweet smile only made me feel worse. I looked around and saw an empty chair behind the guy a few feet away.

"I'll just sit over there. You can have the lounge." I started towards it, but he held up a hand. When I stopped, he grabbed the chair and pulled it closer to the lounge.

"How about I take the chair and you take the lounge? You looked pretty comfortable."

"Thanks." I settled back into the lounge. "I'm Lyss."

"I'm Jem," he said.

"You a fan of the band?" I asked, then cringed. Of course he was. Even if he wasn't, he probably wouldn't say so when it was their party.

Jem arched a brow and chuckled. "I don't think they're too bad. What about you?"

"Their music's good," I agreed with a shrug. My phone pinged, and I glanced at it before putting it back down.

"Do you need to get that?" Jem asked.

I shook my head and put my phone back down. "Just a notification from a client's account."

"What do you do?"

"I'm a social media manager."

"What's that?" Jem's eyebrows scrunched together, giving him a cute, confused look.

Crap. The girls would kill me if I started chatting work while talking with a cute guy. I looked around and quickly found them still chatting and laughing with Ledger.

"You sure you want me to bore you with the details?"

"Positive." He leaned forward and rested his elbows on his knees.

"You asked for it," I sighed. I swung my legs over so I was facing him instead of having to turn my head to look at him. "Social media is one of the best marketing tools, and you have access to it for free. You can pay for ads, but you don't have to if you're doing it right. People are more likely to support and buy from someone that they know, and social media is one way to be seen as a real person. Websites, emails, and things like that have to be professional, and sometimes a little rigid, but you can be a little more relaxed on social media. A lot of people and small businesses get overwhelmed by it, but if you have a schedule for it and do it in small chunks, it's completely doable. Or you get someone like me to do it for you."

"That's interesting."

I laughed. "Hey, I warned you it was boring."

"No, really," Jem insisted. "I didn't realize so much could be done with social media. I've played around with it, but it's a bit over-whelming."

"It can be," I agreed.

A guy walked past carrying a girl who kicked her legs playfully and jokingly telling him to put her down. They were both fresh out of the pool and she flung water on me as they walked by.

"Towel?" Jem offered, holding out the one he had used.

"I'm good." I wiped the droplets off my face with my hand.

"How do you manage different clients?"

"They send me some pictures every week or two, let me know about the sales, promotions, or information they want to highlight, and I organize it and put it on their different social media platforms. Not every social media manager does this, but I also create graphics from scratch so it coordinates with their brand. Colors, fonts, photo filters. It all works together to make a brand cohesive."

"I had no idea there was so much to it." Jem raised his eyebrows, but it seemed more in actual surprise and not like his crazy person alert was blaring in his head.

"Most people don't. I'm just a weirdo who enjoys it." I fiddled with my water bottle and peeled at the wrapper.

"All the greats start out as weirdos that enjoy something. Look at Galileo. His belief that the earth rotated around the sun and not the other way around was considered crazy. People thought he was a weirdo because he enjoyed something and learned more about it."

"Not sure I'm on the same level as Galileo," I said with a laugh. "But thanks."

He smiled and opened his mouth, but Clara plopped down next to me.

"Sorry it took us so long." Clara was talking to me, but her eyes were on the man in front of us. "Glad to see you found some company. Care to introduce us?"

"Sure, I guess." Sheesh, the one guy I'm talking to and Clara pounces on him. Oh, well. I wasn't here looking for a hookup. "Jem, this is Clara. Clara, this—"

"Jasper Tsuji! I'm a huge fan," she interrupted, and stuck her hand out as she gushed.

I looked at Jem, confused. Jasper? Why did that name sound familiar? Thank goodness, I wasn't a cartoon or everyone would have seen the light bulb go off over my head. "You're a member of the band."

Jem smiled sheepishly as Clara gasped.

"He's the one who writes the songs, Lyss," she hissed at me.

"Why didn't you tell me?" I asked, shooting him an accusatory look.

"Do you tell everyone you meet that you're a social media manager?" he asked, arching a brow.

"No," I admitted. I bit my lip and started picking at my thumb nail.

"You got trapped listening to her talk about work?" Clara rolled her eyes and groaned in sympathy. "I'm sorry."

"I enjoyed hearing her insights. I'm still trying to figure out the whole social media thing."

"If that's the case, then Lyss is your girl."

I rolled my eyes as Clara changed her tune. She was so wishy-washy when it came to guys. It drove me nuts when we first started hanging out, but now I just went with it. I knew a quick hip check would give her the signal that she was going over the top. Maybe I'd try not to send her sprawling on the floor like the last time.

Ledger, Gia, and Julie showed up then.

"We're going in the pool. Did you want to join us?" Julie asked me as she pulled her dress over her head to reveal her blue bikini.

My hair tickled my back as I shook my head. "I'm good for now. I'll keep an eye on your drinks, though."

Everyone put their drinks on the small table between mine and Jem's chairs.

"You coming, Jasper?" Clara put one hand on her hip as she asked him, accentuating her curves.

"No, I'm taking a break for a bit."

Clara shrugged and headed to the pool with the others.

"It's too crowded to do anything but stand there," Jem said.

"Don't enjoy standing around in the water?" I asked as I stretched my legs out over the lounger again.

"I prefer swimming if I'm going to be in water."

"I prefer floating," I said. "Get me one of those floaters that has a mesh bottom, so you're still getting wet while you relax, a book, and I'll be set for the afternoon."

"What type of books do you read?" Jem asked.

"Romance. If there's a guy, a girl, and sexual tension, I'll read it."

"Any suggestions?"

I looked at Jem in surprise. "You read romance?"

He shrugged. "Not really, but maybe I just haven't found the right one."

I sat back up and grinned. "Okay, let's start with what spice level you're comfortable with and go from there."

Chapter 2

Lyss

Jem and I chatted about books while the others swam. He revealed he was fine with any spice level as long as there was an actual storyline with it, preferably one with some action. I gave him my favorite authors I thought he would enjoy.

He preferred adventure and horror and gave me a few that he promised I could read and still sleep after.

After books, we started on television shows and discovered we both liked a lot of the same shows.

"Can you tell me where the restroom is?" We had been talking for a while, enough for me to go through another water bottle.

"Yeah, I'll show you. I should go mingle." He grimaced at the idea, making me laugh.

"Sorry to take up so much of your time," I said as we stood up.

"It should be me apologizing to you. You've by far been the best thing of my night." His cheeks darkened as he looked at me from the side of his eye.

"Thanks, you too." I bumped his shoulder. Shyness wasn't what you expected from someone in a band, but it was adorable on him.

I looked for the girls and saw Gia and Julie back in the pool. They had got out earlier and grabbed their drinks before going in search of food. Gia caught my eye, and I made a fist, putting my thumb between my pointer and middle fingers, and shook my hand, giving her the sign language for needing to use the restroom. She gave me a thumbs up and I walked off with Jem.

"The one you can get to from out here has a pretty long line. There's one inside that you can use that should be empty," Jem said.

I bit my lip and looked at the line Jem was referring to. It was pretty long, and I really had to pee.

"I can stand by the door if you want to make sure no one bothers you or I can walk away and leave you be, whichever you're most comfortable with," Jem said when he sensed my hesitation.

A small laugh came out. "I think I'll be okay to use the bathroom by myself, but thanks for the chivalry."

He held up his hands in a placating gesture. "I have a younger sister, so I know girls prefer to go to the bathroom in packs."

"How old is she?" I asked as I followed him into the house.

"She's seventeen now," he said.

"Now?" I asked, needling for more of the story behind that.

"Last time I saw her, she was fourteen."

Three years ago. Right around the time *Sons of Poseidon* came out.

"Parents aren't fans of the rock star lifestyle?" I asked.

"Something like that."

We walked the rest of the way in silence. We probably wouldn't have been able to hear each other if we spoke anyway because of the music being so loud inside the house.

After turning down a hallway, Jem pulled out a key and opened a door leading to a bedroom. I looked at him questioningly.

"It's my room," he explained as he opened the door. "The bathroom is to the right."

He flipped on the light and pointed to the door on the right of the room.

"I'll see you around, Lyss. Just lock the door when you come back out."

"Thanks. See you, Jem."

He closed the door behind me after I walked in. I hurried to the restroom and sighed as my bladder shrank back down to a normal size. I took a minute to reapply my lip gloss and fix my hair after washing my hands. Before leaving the room, I turned off the lights and locked the door, like Jem had requested.

I headed back to the party in search of my friends, dodging between bodies as I made my way back outside.

Julie was talking with a guy where Jem and I had been sitting. Clara and Gia were in the pool playing water volleyball.

"Lyss, you're back!" Clara yelled as she waved wildly at me.

I chuckled and waved back.

"Can you get me another drink? It was a Malibu something," she asked.

I gave her a thumbs up and headed to the bar. The line was short, so I didn't have to wait long.

"Hi, my friend wanted a Malibu something?" I told the bartender, hoping he would know what I was talking about.

"Malibu sunrise," he said right away. "Got it."

He grabbed a tall glass and added ice to it. Then he poured in rum, orange juice, and pineapple juice. He grabbed the grenadine and gently poured it down the side. It settled at the bottom of the glass, finishing the sunset effect. He topped it off with a maraschino cherry and handed it to me.

"Thanks." I smiled and took the glass from him.

My phone buzzed in my pocket. I grabbed it to see what the notification was as I kept walking, and bumped right into someone. I could wander through our apartment scrolling on my phone with no problem, but apparently my party trick didn't work at an actual party.

"Watch it, bitch." The plastic I bumped into pushed me before I could even try apologizing. She definitely wasn't getting one now.

Especially since I tripped over my own foot and ran into someone else.

I held the half empty drink to the side as it dripped off my hand.

A white shirt now had a wet yellowish blob on the front and the man wearing it was annoyed.

"What the hell?" he exclaimed.

I looked up into annoyed eyes and a slight sneer as he held the shirt away from his chest. Just as I opened my mouth to explain, someone shoved me hard between my shoulder blades. With a small shriek, I fell into the man once more. And pushed him into the pool.

My jaw hung open as I watched him find his footing then stand up, flipping his hair out of his face. If he was annoyed before, he was positively pissed now.

"I am so sorry." My eyes were wide while I watched him walk to the edge and lift himself out of the pool. His shirt clung to him and was practically sheer. Water droplets dripped off the edge of his nose and chin. He would definitely win in a wet t-shirt contest. If they had those for guys.

"Watch where you're going," he growled.

"It was an accident," I said. "Someone pushed me."

"Maybe if you weren't on your phone and watching where you were going instead, they wouldn't have needed to push you."

I huffed out a breath and narrowed my eyes. "Well, excuse me, Mr. Perfect. Maybe you should jump back into the pool to cool your attitude. If you don't mind, I'll take my leave now." I bobbed a mocking curtsy before brushing past him.

What a jerk. Who did he think he was? I brought Clara's half empty drink to the pool and waited for her to climb out.

"Wow, did you decide you wanted to drink again?" she asked as she took the drink from me.

"No. I bumped into some asshole who acted like I did it on purpose."

"Was he cute at least?"

I rolled my eyes. "I didn't notice." Lie. I noticed, and he was very cute. Why did attractive guys think they could get away with assholeish tendencies?

Clara shrugged. "Oh, well. Plenty of cute guys here tonight." She looked at the pool and finger waved to some guy that was urging her to come back in.

"Hey, there you are. You doing okay?" Gia came out of the pool to stand by us.

"Yeah, just a little annoyed," I said.

"She spilled my drink on some guy," Clara explained. "And he was a total douche about it."

"But it's done and over with. Moving on now." I pasted a bright smile on. "How's the volleyball game going?"

"I don't think it's as much of a game as it is splashing and missing the ball," Gia said.

"Yeah, it gets funnier the more drunk people are," Clara said. She downed the rest of her drink and handed the empty glass to me. "I should be more fun now."

Gia and I looked at each other and burst out laughing as Clara went back into the pool.

"You're not planning on getting wasted, are you?" I asked.

Gia shook her head. "Nope, one drink is my limit."

"Good, one less person I have to worry about."

A loud giggle had us looking over at Julie. She was laughing loudly at something the guy she was chatting with said. Another guy had joined them at some point.

"Looks like Julie is further along than Clara," Gia said. We both laughed and went back to chatting.

After a few minutes I looked back and noticed Julie and the two guys were gone.

"Do you see Julie?" I asked.

Gia looked around and shook her head. "No, she must have gone inside."

"I'm going to find her and make sure she's okay."

"Want me to come with you?"

I shook my head. "You stay and watch Clara. We don't need her passing out and drowning in the pool."

"Good point. Let me know when you find her."

"I will." I headed towards the house, looking for Julie as I went.

I wandered through the kitchen, TV room, and checked the bedrooms, all of which were locked. I found a set of stairs at the end of a hallway leading to a basement and followed those.

As I neared the bottom of the steps, I could hear low voices. Two male and one female. I peeked into the room, not wanting to interrupt if something was going on that didn't want to be interrupted. It was a large room with weights, a treadmill, and different exercise equipment.

"No."

That was the first word I heard clearly, and I could tell it was Julie, even if it sounded a bit off.

I barged into the room to find one guy standing behind Julie with one arm around her waist to hold her up and one hand cupping her boob over her shirt. The other guy stood in front of her and was pushing her dress up to her waist, exposing her swim bottoms.

"Hey!"

Both the guys jumped and looked at me.

"This room's taken. Give us about fifteen minutes and you can have it," one of them said.

"How about I have the room now?" I put my hands on my hips and stared them down.

The guy holding Julie from behind looked at his friend and transferred Julie into his grip. His smile was smug and creepy as he walked towards me.

"If you wanted to join in on the fun, all you had to do was ask." He reached out to touch my face, but I slapped his hand away.

"Don't touch me. And you"—I looked around the guy in front of me to the other guy—"put her down and quit touching her."

"But she likes it, don't you, Jules?" He pulled her closer and kissed her cheek.

Julie pushed weakly against his chest. I glared at the guy closest to me.

"What the hell did you give her?"

"Don't worry about it, gorgeous." He stepped closer and snaked an arm out to wrap around my waist.

"Let go," I demanded. I pushed at him and when that didn't work, I slapped him across the face. The crack of it sounded through the room and his head whipped to the side.

His grip on me only tightened as he turned his head back to look at me. The smile he had worn was now replaced with a sneer. One of his hands reached up to grab my hair, and he pulled on it, forcing my head back. I yelped at the sting and he smashed his lips onto mine.

I bit down hard. He pulled back and let go of my hair to wipe the back of his hand across his mouth. A bit of blood smeared across his chin and I grinned in satisfaction that I had hurt him.

"I like them with a bit of bite," he said, the creepy grin returning. "But yours is a little much for my taste. Maybe you need a lesson on how to behave."

"I think you're the one that needs the lesson." I lifted my knee, but he blocked it from making contact with where I wanted it to.

He laughed and pushed me backwards until my back slammed against the wall. He nudged his knee between my legs and pressed his hips against mine, then held my hands next to my head, pinning me to the wall.

"Julie!" I called out as I bucked against the man pinning me down.

"She's so wasted she probably doesn't know her own name." The guy laughed in my face.

I screamed as loud as I could and continued thrashing.

Suddenly the weight was pulled off me and I fell forward into a pair of arms.

"Lyss, Lyss. It's okay, it's Jem. Are you alright?" He took a step back as soon as I was steady.

"Julie, where's Julie?" I looked around for my friend.

16

"She's fine. Ledger's helping her."

As soon as he said that, I saw Ledger punch the guy who had been with Julie in the stomach. The guy grunted and doubled over. Julie scooted backwards away from the two men. I rushed to her and fell to the ground next to her.

"Are you okay?" I asked my friend. I pushed her hair back and looked into her bloodshot, tear-filled eyes.

She nodded and grabbed onto my forearms.

"I didn't want to. They didn't listen to me," she sobbed.

"You're okay now." I pulled her into a hug and stroked her hair. "You're safe."

"Are you girls okay?" Ledger knelt next to us and looked at us with concern in his eyes.

I nodded and gave him a small smile.

Now that I knew Julie was alright, I paid attention to what was going on around me.

A mountain of a man with a buzz cut and close-cropped beard was wailing on the guy that had assaulted me. Jem tried to pull him off of the limp molester, but the man just pushed him away with a large hand, making Jem stumble back. I turned back to Julie.

"I'm going to leave you with Ledger for just a minute," I told her.

"Where are you going?" Julie tightened her grip on me.

I looked at Ledger and he nodded, reaching out to hold Julie's hand. She looked at him then back at me questioningly.

"I'm going to go help jackass over there." I motioned with my head to where the creep was still getting wailed on.

"Looks like he's getting plenty of help," Ledger said casually, as if he wasn't bothered that the guy was getting beaten to a pulp in front of us.

"I'll be back," I told Julie once more before I jumped up and ran to the creep and the guy beating the shit out of him.

"Whoa, what are you doing?" Jem grabbed my arm when I tried to walk past him.

"Stopping that." I pointed to the one-way fight still going on.

Jem shook his head. "No way. Rook might end up hurting you."

Ah, Rook Huxley, the silent, and apparently deadly, bass player of the band. He was even bigger than his pictures made him look.

"Someone has to stop him," I said.

"I think that guy is getting what he deserves.

My eyes opened wide at the vehemence in Jem's tone.

"He's a stupid, chauvinistic creep, but he doesn't deserve to die," I said.

Jem didn't say anything else, but he let go of my arm.

I approached Rook from the side so he could see me.

"Hey," I said gently. I put my hand on the big guy's shoulder.

He shrugged, but I didn't move my hand.

"Thank you for beating this creep, but I think he learned his lesson," I said softly, kneeling down next to Rook.

The creep's face was a mess. His eye was already swelling shut and his lip was split.

"Rook, you're scaring, Lyss," Jem said from behind me.

Rook lowered his raised fist and let go of the creep's shirt. A groan sounded from him as his head hit the floor. Rook finally turned his gaze to me. He looked me up and down, as if making sure I was okay.

"I'm okay, big guy," I kept my voice low and soft, trying to sound soothing.

"No bitch is worth this," the creep said.

Holy shit, the guy was still conscious after all that?

Rook turned back to the guy and sucker punched him, knocking him out cold. He looked back at me and I just shrugged.

"Eh, he was kinda asking for it. Some people need to learn when to keep their mouths shut." I stood up and toed the creep to see if he was really out.

"Get your friend and get out of here," Rook growled at the other guy.

"Wait," I said. I walked right up to the guy that had been touching one of my best friends and got in his face. "What did you give her?"

"Nothing, honest." He held his hands up placatingly. "She was just super wasted and said she was down for some fun."

"That's why she was saying no when I got down here and you kept going?" I scoffed. "Leave before I let these guys loose on you again."

He ran past me to his friend, who started to move. He helped him up, and they both limped up the stairs and out of the room.

I knelt next to Julie and helped her up.

"I got her, little guppy," Rook said. He looked at me for permission first, and I nodded my head. He scooped Julie up like she weighed nothing.

"Thank you guys for showing up when you did," I said.

"I wish we would have got here sooner," Ledger said as he glared at the now empty stairwell.

"How did you know we were down here?" I asked.

"I couldn't find you, so I asked one of your friends. She said you were looking for Julie and seemed a bit worried," Jem said.

"You were looking for me?" I smiled.

He scratched the back of his neck and his cheeks pinked up again. "I, uh, just wanted to make sure you were having a good time."

I nodded my head, but decided not to call him out on his lame excuse. It was sweet of him and I liked that he wanted to find me again.

"What should we do about Julie?" Ledger asked.

"I'll order us an Uber and we'll head home," I said. I pulled out my phone to open the app.

"Why don't you girls stay here tonight?" Ledger asked.

"Yeah, Julie is already asleep," Jem said.

I looked over at my friend and sure enough, she was lightly snoring.

"Clara was three kelps to the current last time I saw her," Jem added.

"Kelps to the current?" I raised an eyebrow at the odd phrase.

"He means wasted," Ledger said. "So, how about it, doll?"

I chewed on my lower lip and looked at my phone. It would be an hour or so before we got home between waiting for an Uber and the drive back to our place. I wasn't sure if Gia and I could get Julie and Clara both up two flights of stairs to our apartment. And I was exhausted. Working the breakfast shift this morning and being up this late, any energy I had from the borrowed adrenaline of the party was fading fast.

"You're sure you don't mind?" I asked, looking at each man.

"Not a problem," Jem assured me. "Let me show you where you guys can stay."

Chapter 3

Lyss

I followed Jem up the stairs, with Rook and Julie behind us. Ledger had gone ahead of us to find Gia and Clara and let them know what was going on.

Jem led us to a room across from his and opened it. It was plain, no wall decor or little touches, that someone lived here, but there was a king sized bed in the middle.

"It's the guest room, but no one ever uses it. Will it be okay?" Jem asked.

"It's perfect," I said.

Rook came in and I pulled the covers back so he could lay Julie down.

"I'm going to kick everyone else out," Rook said.

"You don't have to kick them out for us. Julie doesn't budge once she's asleep," I said. I unbuckled Julie's sandals and slid them off her feet before covering her with the blankets.

"What happened to you two shouldn't have happened. The party is over." Rook walked out of the room and closed the door behind him.

I looked at Jem with a raised brow.

"He's not much of a people person," Jem said with a grin. "If it wasn't this, he would have come up with another reason soon. I'll let you get situated. Just yell for me if you need anything." Jem left the room, leaving me alone with a snoring Julie.

Well, it was their party, not mine. I finished tucking Julie in. A few minutes later, Gia and Clara came in.

"We're having a sleepover with *Sons of Poseidon!*" Clara squealed and clapped her hands.

"She snuck another drink when I wasn't looking," Gia said by way of explanation.

"Makes sense," I said.

"What happened? Ledger came and found us and told us something went down, but he wouldn't say what. Are you okay? Is Julie?" She looked over my shoulder at Julie.

"We're fine. Now."

"What about before now?" Gia asked.

Clara was singing a Dua Lipa song and dancing around the room.

"I haven't heard Julie's side of the story, but apparently she went a little overboard with the drinking too and told those guys she was talking to that she wanted to have some fun. I found them in the basement and heard her telling them no, but they weren't listening." My hands squeezed into fists as I remembered.

Gia gasped and turned pale. "Did they—?"

I shook my head. "No, I stopped them before it got that far. The guys showed up not long after. Rook beat the shit out of the one that started harassing me when I interrupted them." I didn't mention that I had found myself in a similar position to Julie.

"Whose bed do you think this is?" Clara asked. She fell face first onto it and had her arms spread wide, like she was trying to hug it. "It smells like Jasper! I mean, Jem. He said I could call him Jem."

Gia and I looked at each other and started laughing as Clara rubbed her face on the bed.

A knock sounded at the door and I opened it.

"I brought you girls some t-shirts to sleep in," Jem said.

"Thanks, Jem." I smiled warmly at him as I took the shirts.

"There should be towels in the bathroom if you need them, as well as shampoo and stuff. I doubt it's what you would normally use, but—"

"Whatever it is will be fine. Thank you," I reassured him.

"Alright, well, I'm just across the hall if you need me."

I thanked him again and closed the door.

"I call shower first," Gia said as soon as the door closed. She grabbed the t-shirt on top and headed to the bathroom. She hated the feel of chlorine on her skin after swimming.

"Clara, how about we get you out of your wet clothes and into something more comfortable?" I suggested.

"Are those Jem's shirts?" Her eyes opened wide as she looked at the shirt I held up.

"Yeah." At least I assumed so, since he's the one that brought them to me.

It took her all of two seconds to strip out of her bikini and grab the shirt. She put it on and wrapped her arms around herself.

"This was on his bare skin and now it's on mine!" She twirled in a circle, bumped into the bed, and fell to the floor.

I snorted a laugh, then helped her up.

"Let's get you into bed so you can sleep this off," I said.

"I'm not feeling very good," she mumbled.

I grabbed the wastebasket that was next to the bed and put it in front of her just in time.

I rubbed her back and held back strands of her hair that had fallen from her bun while she emptied her stomach in the small container.

"What the hell did I drink?" she asked when she was done.

"I believe it was a Malibu sunrise." I patted her back and stood up. "I'm going to get some water for you. Think you'll be alright?"

"Yeah, I'm done. I just need to sleep now."

"Let's change your shirt because you got some grossness on this one."

23

She looked down at the shirt and started to cry. "I defiled his shirt."

I bit the inside of my cheek to keep from laughing. "It's okay. I'll get it washed and he'll never know."

"You're the best, Lyss." Clara lifted her arms, and I pulled off her dirty shirt and put a new one on. She crawled into bed as Gia came out of the bathroom, steam pouring out after her.

"Did she do her puking and crying?" Gia gestured towards Clara with a jut of her chin while she rubbed lotion on her arms.

"Yup. She got puke on Jem's shirt and said she defiled it."

Gia laughed and shook her head. "That girl."

"I'm going to get water and some ibuprofen for when they wake up. And see if I can wash her clothes. Do you want me to throw yours in too?"

"That would be great." She grabbed her bikini and dress from the bathroom.

I gathered the clothes in my arms and was almost out the door when I turned back to Gia. "Can you empty Clara's puke bucket? Love you, G," I closed the door before she could yell at me.

The house was oddly quiet. I was impressed at how quickly Rook had gotten everyone to leave. I knocked on Jem's door and he answered immediately.

"Everything alright?" he asked.

"I had a couple more favors to ask." I winced and held up the clothes. "Is there anyway I can wash these? Clara's drinking always ends the same way, puking, crying, and passing out."

Jem laughed and motioned for me to follow him. He led me to the laundry room, and I threw everything into the washing machine.

"Um, you have some..." He pointed to my shorts.

I looked down and saw that some of Clara's backsplash had landed on me, too. I crinkled my nose and sighed.

"Let me grab another t-shirt you can change into so you can wash those too."

I waited while he ran back to his room and returned with a t-shirt.

"I'll just..." He pointed behind him with his thumb and stood in the hall, closing the door behind him.

His awkward moments were seriously adorable. I stripped out of my clothes and threw them in with the rest of the clothes. I kept my underwear and bra on, and pulled his shirt over my head. I added laundry soap and started the wash.

Jem was still waiting for me when I opened the door.

"Do you guys need water or anything?" he asked.

"Yeah, and ibuprofen if you have any."

"Of course."

We walked to the kitchen. He pulled a few water bottles out of the fridge and set them on the counter.

"Hey, doll. You guys getting settled in alright?" Ledger came in and snagged a bag of chips from a cupboard and popped a chip into his mouth. It was green. I looked at the bag and saw sea salt seaweed written on it. Must be some diet thing. No one actually liked that stuff, did they?

"Yeah, I'm just making sure everyone is taken care of." A huge yawn caught me off guard and my jaw popped because I opened my mouth so wide. "Wow, I'm so sorry. Guess the day is catching up with me."

"Didn't you say you worked a morning shift today?" Ledger asked.

I nodded my head.

Ledger walked closer to me and studied my face. He reached out and gently traced his thumb under my eye.

"You look exhausted."

"You're not supposed to tell a girl that." I smiled to show I was teasing. "I am, but I have to put the clothes over to dry after they wash, bring the girls water and ibuprofen for when they wake up—"

"We can do that," Jem interrupted. "You should just go rest."

If these guys were insisting, I wasn't going to fight it. "Do you have an extra pillow and blanket?"

"Is it not warm enough?" Jem asked.

"It is, but Julie, Clara, and Gia are on the bed, so I was just going to lie on the floor to give them more room."

"You're not sleeping on the floor."

I jumped at the voice coming from behind me.

"Rook, I didn't even hear you come in," I said.

"He's part ninja," Ledger said.

"You can use my room," Rook said.

I shook my head. "You guys have already done so much for us, I can't take your room. I'm fine on the floor, honest. At this point, I would be fine sleeping outside on one of the lounge chairs."

"Which is why you'll use my room. I won't be home tonight, anyway." Rook looked at Ledger and Jem. "Dorian and I are heading out."

The fourth and final member of *Sons of Poseidon*, Dorian Verlice. Lead singer and the only one I haven't met tonight.

"We're good here," Jem said.

Rook nodded and went out the back door.

"I'll take these to the girls," Jem said, gesturing to the waters and ibuprofen. "Ledger, will you show Lyss where Rook's room is?"

"Yes, sir." Ledger gave him a cheesy salute.

I followed Ledger and instead of turning right towards Jem's and the guest room, he turned left. He opened a door, and we walked in. The bed was neatly made and everything seemed to have a place and be in its place.

"I'm kinda worried I'll mess something up in here," I said.

Ledger chuckled. "Rook does like his organization, but I promise you won't mess anything up enough to make him upset. Besides, that's my job."

I yawned again.

"Get to bed, doll."

I nodded and crawled into the bed, snuggling under the covers. Once I was situated, Ledger closed the door, surrounding me in darkness.

A few minutes later, the door opened, and I squinted to see who it was.

"Lyss, are you in here?"

"Gia?" I sat up. "What's going on?"

"Jem said you were sleeping in another room and, given everything that's happened tonight, I wanted to make sure you were alright."

"You're the best," I said. "I'm good, promise. Rook won't even be home tonight. When I asked for an extra pillow and blanket so I could sleep on the floor, he offered me his room."

"For sexy musicians they're sure accommodating, aren't they? You'll be okay by yourself?" Gia asked.

"I'm great. I was almost asleep when you came in. If it makes you feel better, you can sleep in here too."

"I should stay with Julie and Clara so they don't freak when they wake up and don't know where they're at. Besides, you're a bed hog."

"Well, you're a blanket hog, so probably a good thing anyway," I teased.

Gia laughed. "Night, Lyss."

"Night, G."

She closed the door, and I was out almost immediately after my head hit the pillow.

Chapter 4

Lyss

The best part of waking up without an alarm is the different stages. First there's the dream stage. You're still dreaming, but you're recognizing that it's not real. Then the dream flickers in and out of reality. You wrap yourself deeper into your blankets, trying to stay asleep. You keep your eyes close and feel how heavenly your bed feels. Reality becomes reality once more, and you're ready for a new day.

Sometimes that euphoria fades quickly when reality is no fun to be in, other times you can ride that feeling for a while. Today was the latter.

The door opened and blinded me briefly with the bright light that came through. I sat up, keeping the covers pulled to my chest, and squinted to see who it was.

"Did I wake you up?" Rook stood in the doorway, not coming in yet.

"No, I woke up a couple of minutes ago." I stretched my arms over my head and heard my back pop a couple times. "I'll get out of your way so you can have your bed back."

"No rush. I was just going to jump in the shower." He opened a dresser drawer and pulled out a couple of items before asking, "Did you sleep okay?"

"I slept amazing," I said. "Thank you for letting me use your room."

"I made breakfast. It's in the kitchen if you want some."

"Awesome! Thank you so much for doing that." I kicked the covers off and jumped out of the bed. I pulled the covers back up and fluffed the pillows. When I turned around, Rook was watching me. I tucked my hair behind my ear and prayed it wasn't sticking up everywhere. "Sorry, would you prefer I strip the bed to wash the sheets?"

"No." He walked into the bathroom and closed the door.

He was a man of few words, but I think I liked it. I knew whatever he said was what he meant. Now to find that breakfast.

As I left Rook's room, the door across from his opened and a familiar guy walked out. One that had flipped out when I spilled a drink on him. This must be Dorian. Great.

"You." His lip lifted in a sneer.

I forced a smile that felt more like baring my teeth. He and his friends were kind enough to let the girls and I stay the night. The least I could do was play nice.

He started walking away, and I hurried after him.

"Wait." I put a hand on his arm to stop him.

He stopped and looked down his nose at my hand on his bicep with a glare. I dropped my hand.

"I wanted to apologize for yesterday," I said. "I should have been paying more attention to my surroundings."

"No problem, Amaryllis," he said snidely, and walked off.

I stood frozen for a second before snapping my hands to my hips. "What did you just call me?"

"Did you say something, Amaryllis?" he called over his shoulder, not pausing for a second.

I ran to catch up with him again and grabbed his arm again. He stopped and sneered down at my hand like he did last time, but instead of letting go, I just squeezed harder. Hot damn, this boy was packing some muscle. I fought the urge to examine the rest of his bicep and glared up at him.

"What did you call me?" I repeated my question.

His sneer turned into a cocky smirk. "Trouble with your hearing as well as your eyes, *Amaryllis*?"

"I prefer to be called Lyss," I said through clenched teeth. "Who told you my name was Amaryllis?"

"It's amazing the things you can find on the internet," he said.

"What? Did you *Google* me?"

"Haven't you Googled *me*?"

Damn him. Of course I had. And I had even admitted it to Jem, which probably was who told this jerk.

"Are we done?" Dorian asked. He crossed his arms, making his bicep feel even bigger. I refused to let go, though. That would show weakness in front of an enemy, which is what he was if he didn't get my name right.

"Yeah, we're done, Dory."

"What did you call me?"

I tilted my head to the side and smiled. "What? You can dish it, but can't take it? Poor Dory." I patted his arm and headed towards the kitchen and the delicious smell of bacon and pancakes.

"That's a fish's name," he called.

"And now it's yours," I said and waved to him without turning around.

"Hey, Lyss. Want some coffee?" Jem asked, holding up a mug of his own coffee. Now that his hair was dry, and the sun was out, I saw he had streaks of red throughout his dark hair.

I scrunched up my nose and took a seat at the counter. "I'm not much of a coffee drinker. Do you have any hot chocolate?"

"Maybe? Let me check." He set his mug down and went to the pantry.

"If I had known you were up, I would have asked if you wanted a shower." Ledger walked into the room, his blond hair dark from being still wet. "I could have helped you wash your back. I've been told I'm excellent in all things wet and slippery."

"I'm sure your hand found wet and slippery just fine in there." I patted his knee and hopped off my seat. Jem had pulled out a mug and a canister of hot chocolate and set it on the counter for me.

Ledger roared with laughter. "You have some spice in you, doll."

"Sugar, spice, and all things nice." I winked at him as I filled up the kettle with water.

Dorian snorted. "Nursery rhymes, no alcohol, and no coffee. Sure you don't want a juice box, Amaryllis?"

I put the kettle on the stove before staring at Dorian with my arms crossed. "Ledger? Would you mind asking Dory why he insists on being such a dick when I've already apologized for bruising his little ego?"

Jem and Ledger remained silent while Dorian's eyes narrowed into slits. Red was working its way up his neck. Dorian stared me down, and I stared right back. Finally, he growled and stood up.

"Jem, bring me breakfast in my room. I'll be there until *Amaryllis* is gone."

Oh, it was on. I would not be pushed around by some self-entitled asshole just because I got his shirt a little dirty. "He's not your servant! You can't just boss him around like that." I stomped around the island to yell at him.

Ledger and Jem exchanged a look, but I barely noticed it because I was so focused on the asshole in front of me.

"I can do what I want," he declared. "This is my house, not yours. You're barely even a guest here. If it wasn't for these three, you wouldn't even be here. Now you're here eating our food, wearing our clothes, and insulting me. *After* ruining my favorite shirt."

"Fine. I'll leave." I turned to the other three men. "Thank you so much for your hospitality. I'm so sorry that I've been such a burden. I wish you the best, and I wish you"—I turned back to Dorian—"a front-row seat in hell."

31

"That's a special edition t-shirt. You're not taking it with you," Dorian said after I walked past him.

I smiled as I grabbed the hem of the shirt, pulled it over my head, balled it up and shoved it into Dorian's chest. "Wouldn't dream of taking it, Dory."

With that final word, I held my head high and walked off.

After I rounded the corner and was out of view of the guys, I stopped to take a couple deep breaths to calm down before I woke up the girls.

A loud smack sounded behind me.

"What the hell, dickhead?" Dorian growled.

I grinned. Sounded like one of the boys had smacked him upside the head. Served him right.

"Why were you acting that way with Lyss? She's not going to want to hang out with us if—" Another smack and Ledger stopped speaking.

"We're not discussing this right now." I could hardly make out Jem's low command.

They were worried about me not hanging out with them? Why would they care? Were they worried I'd post something about Dorian being a dick on social media? Even if I did, I would probably just be attacked saying I was being uptight or deserved the way he treated me. Yay for social media trolls and anti-feminism.

The boys lowered their voices, and I tiptoed near the wall to get as close as I could without being seen around the corner. As I listened to their mumbles, I failed to hear Jem walking to me. I gasped when he rounded the corner and almost ran into me.

"Eavesdropping, Lyss?" His smile told me he didn't really care.

I peeked around the corner to see if the guys had heard him and they were all staring at us. Busted.

"Nope, I thought I dropped an earring, but then I remembered I didn't wear any, so it's all good."

Jem snorted. "All good," he agreed, shaking his head. "I switched your laundry over to dry last night. Should still be in the dryer."

Damn. That was on the other side of the hall. I'd have to walk past the guys in my underwear again.

"Is it okay with his highness that I take the time to get dressed before I leave?" I asked.

A smirk graced Jem's face. "I have a feeling he doesn't have much say in the matter."

I returned his smile and went to the laundry room. I kept my chin high and my eyes straight when I had to pass in front of the living room and kitchen again.

"Damn, that girl has a nice ass," Ledger muttered after I walked by.

I bit my lip to keep from grinning like an idiot. The playboy rock star thought I had a nice ass. Not gonna lie, that was a decent boost to the ego.

I gathered our clothes from the dryer, putting them in a basket and carried them back to the guest room.

Jem came out of his room again. I put the basket down and wrapped my arms around his waist. He stood frozen for a moment before returning the hug.

"What's this for?" he asked. "Not that I'm complaining in the slightest."

"For not trying to get into my pants or being an asshole."

"Not that I don't want to," he muttered.

"What was that?" I leaned back to look up at him.

"To get into your pants, not be an asshole," he clarified quickly. The realization of what he said hit him, and his face turned bright red. "I mean, sorry, that's not what I meant. I respect you. You're beautiful, but I don't want in your pants. Well, I wouldn't say no, but that's totally your decision."

I burst out laughing and covered his mouth with my hand to get him to stop talking. The poor guy was bright red now.

"Thank you." I let go of him and opened the door. As I stepped into the room, I turned back. "I wouldn't say no either."

I closed the door behind me on his embarrassed smirk. How was he so sweet after hanging around his asshole of a friend so often?

* * *

Jem

"I think I'm in love. I vote we keep her," Ledger said when I walked back into the kitchen.

"We can't keep her. She's not a plaything." I didn't disagree with him, though. I didn't know where to put my hands when she gave me that hug in only her bra and panties, but there were a hundred places I wanted to put them. Even now, I could feel the warmth of her arms around my waist. And the softness of her front pressed against mine.

"Did you see the way she threw her shirt at Dorian?" Ledger roared with laughter.

"It wasn't her shirt," Dorian mumbled.

"It also wasn't a special edition," Rook said. Dorian glared at him and I hid my smile in my coffee.

"Damn, that girl has a body." Ledger leaned on the counter and looked dreamy.

"I'm going to take a shower." Dorian pushed off his chair.

"Wait," I said.

Dorian stopped, and I knew I had about ten seconds to speak.

"We still good about hiring her as our social media manager?" I asked.

I had brought up the idea last night and everyone seemed on board with the idea, but I wanted to be sure before bringing it up to her.

"No." Dorian shook his head. "Not happening."

"Why?" I knew he wouldn't have a good reason.

"She spilled her drink on me, then pushed me into the pool," he said, pointing towards the back yard.

Ledger laughed at that. "Is your pride really that wounded over a little dip in the water?"

Dorian glared at him, but didn't say anything back.

I turned my attention to Ledger and Rook. "What do you guys think?"

"I say 'hell yeah!'" Ledger said.

Rook looked at Dorian, then frowned as he thought. "Do we really need a social media manager? We've been doing fine on our own so far."

"Not really. Since firing our last PR guy, our numbers have been dropping. There's a lot more to it than I thought there would be, and I just don't have the time to deal with it," I explained again with a weary sigh. We had gone over it last night. I was drowning in this whole social media/marketing madness. "With taking the year off, we need someone to help keep up the momentum we've gained. People want to see us as real people, not these super secretive rock stars."

"Who knows if we'll even still be doing this after the year is up," Dorian said.

"We don't, but I think we can all agree we enjoy living up here. I can learn from her, so if it doesn't work out, I can hopefully keep us afloat. Even if you have other priorities, I'm sure you'll occasionally want to come back. This provides us with a stream of income, so we can sneak away unnoticed." I might be stretching for a reason, but it was a pretty good one. Plus, I wanted Lyss around. There was something about her that did something to me. I wasn't even sure what it did, but I liked it.

"There's a reason we've been super secretive," Rook pointed out. He was mixing up more pancake batter to cook up. Ledger had already inhaled half the stack he had made, and the girls hadn't eaten yet. "And human girls eat that shit up."

"Not so loud." I looked over my shoulder, half expecting all the girls to be standing there and wondering why Rook was talking about *human* girls.

Rook rolled his eyes. "They can't hear us in here, Jem."

35

They better not. I didn't want to freak Lyss out before she had a chance to get to know us.

"If we're getting someone to post behind-the-scenes shit, they're going to be around us a lot. We need someone we can trust and someone who will spend their time here. I doubt she would want to spend half her time driving back and forth between our place and hers. And didn't you say they live on the other side of town? That's a twenty minute drive with Ledger driving, at least forty-five minutes for anyone else." Dorian smiled smugly, thinking he had finally come up with a good reason to not hire her.

He was right. Whoever it was going to be would spend a lot of time here. We could trust Lyss though, I knew we could. My gut was telling me she was the right choice and my gut hadn't been wrong yet.

"Then we ask her to move in," I said.

Dorian looked at me like I just grew an extra tail.

I shrugged. "Like you said, she would spend a lot of time driving, plus what if we have an event that's early or late? It would be easier if she were here."

"He's making sense," Ledger said.

"You just want her here so you can get into her pants." Dorian shot Ledger a pointed look.

Ledger grinned and shrugged, not bothering to deny it.

"We can't pounce on her if she's working for us." As much as I hated to say it. Now, if she made a move, that was a different story.

"Especially if Ledger ends up disappointing her and makes her leave," Rook said. He put fresh bacon into the pan, making it sizzle.

"What happens if she finds out while she's living here?" Dorian asked, trying to find another argument against her.

"We be careful, just like we have been. Swims at night or after taking the boat out far enough that no one can see us," I said.

"Let's put it to a vote, all in favor of getting Lyss to stick around?" Ledger raised his hand, and I followed suit. Dorian crossed his arms and stared us both down. Without even looking at us, Rook raised his left hand in the air while he flipped a pancake with his right.

"The ayes have it." Ledger pumped his fist into the air.

"Dorian?" Rook looked at the man that could veto it regardless of the voting if he really wanted to.

"Fine, but you guys deal with her." Dorian turned and walked to his room.

"She'll grow on him," Ledger said.

I shook my head. "I don't think that's the problem." Dorian was cordial to almost everybody, it was part of his job description. For him to be pushing this hard against Lyss already, there had to be something pulling at him just as strongly as it was for the rest of us.

"What? You think he won't ever like her?"

"I think he already does, and that's what he doesn't like."

Chapter 5

Lyss

The door to the guest room was silent as I opened it and went in. Gia was hugging one edge with her arm, head thrown over the side. Julie was curled up in a ball on the other edge, and Clara starfished in the middle, snoring. I giggled and set the basket of our clothes down. I dug out my clothes and put them on.

While the girls still slept, I went into the ensuite bathroom to relieve my very full bladder. I poked around the drawers and found a stash of toothbrushes in individual packaging and travel-sized toothpastes. Dorian might get mad at me for using more of their stuff, but oh well. It surprised me that any of the guys got within ten feet of me with this dragon breath. I did a quick rinse of my face and I felt almost normal.

"Wakey, wakey," I sang as I stepped out of the bathroom. I flipped on the light and grinned when Gia and Julie groaned. Clara was still snoring away, oblivious to the world.

"What time is it?" Julie croaked.

"About seven," I replied.

"In the morning? Come get me in about five hours." Gia pulled a pillow over her head.

"You can nap at our apartment. We need to get going." I sorted through the laundry basket and separated their outfits at the foot of the bed.

"Ugh, fine. I can't sleep with Clara's snoring, anyway." Gia grabbed her pillow and threw it at Clara's face.

Clara snorted and sat up. "Whatever it was, it wasn't me."

That got the other three of us laughing. Clara looked around, confused, before joining in as she realized she must have been dreaming. They slowly made their way out of the bed and took turns using the bathroom and getting dressed.

I pulled Julie to the side while Clara was in the bathroom, since she still didn't know what had happened.

"Hey, how are you doing?" I asked gently.

She groaned. "This headache is a bitch."

"Do you... remember much of last night?" I asked.

Her eyebrows furrowed as she thought back. "I remember getting here. Ledger getting us in so you didn't bail on us."

I rolled my eyes. It's not like I had wanted to leave just for the hell of it.

"We got drinks, hung out in the pool." Julie rubbed her forehead. I grabbed the still unopened water and ibuprofen that was on the nightstand next to her. I shook out two pills and opened the water bottle before handing them to her.

"Thanks." She took the items gratefully and swallowed the pills before drinking half the water.

"What else do you remember?" Gia sat on the other side of Julie and rubbed her back.

"I was sitting where you had been," Julie looked at me. "And some guy came over to talk. He was really sweet and really cute. He got us both drinks. His friend joined us and brought more drinks. Something felt off about him, but he was nice enough, so I figured I was being paranoid."

Gia and I sat while Julie took another drink of water.

"They asked if I was up for something fun and I told them sure. I was pretty out of it by that point. I remember having to lean on the nice one while we walked. We went down some stairs to a gym, I think?" A frown appeared, and she started fidgeting with her water bottle. "The creepy one started touching me. I told him no, but they just laughed." Tears filled her eyes, and I wrapped an arm through hers.

"I called him the creepy one, too," I whispered.

"You were there." Julie looked at me. "I didn't make that part up?"

I shook my head.

"Lyss was the one to notice you were gone," Gia said. "She went looking for you."

"Thank you." Julie wrapped her arms around me.

"You know we got your back," I said as I patted hers. "Gia would have been there with me, but Clara was already three kelps to the current."

Julie pulled back to look at me funny. Gia mirrored her expression.

"It's what the guys said last night. I thought it was funny and kinda cute, given their name." I shrugged my shoulders.

Gia and Julie shrugged their shoulders too and started laughing.

"What's so funny?" Clara came out of the bathroom, still towel drying her hair.

"You, being three kelps to the current," Gia said.

Clara looked at us like we were crazy and we dissolved into giggles again.

With a shrug, Clara spied the ibuprofen and got two, chewing them.

"How can you do that?" Julie asked, looking a little green.

"Gets in your system faster," Clara said. "Do you think Jem will let me keep his shirt?"

"I have no idea, but they have breakfast ready for us," I said.

"Why are we still in here, then?" Clara looked in the mirror, fluffed her hair, and walked out the door.

Gia gave Julie's back one last rub before following Clara.

"Lyss," Julie said when I stood up.

I looked at her and waited for her to talk.

"How did you get those guys to leave?"

"Jem, Ledger, and Rook showed up right after I did. Rook beat the shit out of the creepy one and Ledger took care of the other guy."

Julie nodded. "Then they let us stay here?"

"Yeah. The musician stereotype doesn't seem to fit them very well, does it?" Except for Dorian. He pulled the asshole, holier-than-thou crap off really well.

When we got to the kitchen, Ledger, Rook, and Jem were eating breakfast at the island, but Dorian was nowhere to be seen. Thank goodness.

"Good morning, you gorgeous girls. Want some breakfast?" Ledger popped up from his seat and pulled four plates out of a cupboard.

Gia, Clara, and Julie happily agreed and grabbed a plate. I sat down next to Rook on the edge of the island.

"The water should still be hot if you want your hot chocolate," Rook said.

I smiled brightly and patted his arm before getting up to make a cup.

"You and your hot chocolate," Gia groaned. "Is there anything stronger around here?"

"Coffee?" Jem asked.

The three girls agreed eagerly, and he poured them each a cup. After handing them their coffees, he went to the fridge and brought out several flavors of creamer. Clara and Julie both opted for plain vanilla, but Gia grabbed the pumpkin spice.

I finished making my hot chocolate and grabbed the hazelnut creamer. There wasn't much left, so I poured the rest of it in. Ledger snickered, and I looked at him suspiciously.

"What? Is it expired?" I looked at the bottle for the expiration date.

41

"Not at all. It just happens to be Dorian's favorite, and you just used the last of it."

Oops.

"And he hasn't had his coffee this morning yet," Jem chimed in.

With any luck, we'd be gone before he came back out. I leaned against the counter and sipped my hot chocolate.

As if the devil himself had heard my thoughts and wanted to stir up shit, Dorian came back out.

He smiled at the girls. "How did you all sleep? Was the bed comfortable?"

My jaw dropped. Where was that stunning hospitality when I was out here this morning?

All three of my friends simped and smiled as they answered Dorian. He grabbed a mug and filled up on coffee while continuing to chat with my friends. All while ignoring me. Knowing I would have my revenge, even if it wasn't on purpose, I just stood quietly and waited.

"Where's the hazelnut?" Dorian asked as he looked through the bottles of creamer on the counter. He went to the fridge to check there.

"Oh, are you a hazelnut fan too?" I asked innocently.

Dorian closed the refrigerator door slowly.

"If I had known, I wouldn't have put the last of it in my delicious hot chocolate," I continued.

Dorian turned to glare at me. I sipped my drink loudly and licked my lips with a hum of satisfaction.

"I hate to eat and run, but I have to work in about three hours and I need at least half of that to soak in the shower to get rid of this headache." Julie broke through mine and Dorian's stare down.

"I can give you guys a ride," Jem offered.

"Are you sure? We can call an Uber or something," Clara said.

"And miss spending extra time with you lovely ladies?" Ledger draped one arm around Clara and one arm around Gia. "Not a chance."

Clara giggled, and Gia turned bright red. Our shoes and purses were waiting for us in a closet near the front door. I remembered I had never properly thanked Rook for his help last night and hurried back to the kitchen while Ledger escorted the other three out the front door.

Rook was still at the island, flicking his finger across the screen on his phone. I wrapped my arms around his neck in a hug. His hand came up and grabbed mine. Next thing I know, I'm standing with my arm twisted behind my back, pressed tightly against Rook's front, and his other arm across my stomach, holding me firm.

"Shit! I'm so sorry, Lyss." Rook immediately let go of me and stepped away.

"You're fine. I guess I know not to sneak up on you now, right?" I forced out a chuckle as I rubbed my wrist.

"Aw, did Amaryllis hurt herself?"

I glared at Dorian. Why, oh, why did he have such an unhealthy obsession with my full name? Maybe he wanted to be kicked in the balls. Yeah, that had to be it.

"I'm fine. I just wanted to thank Rook for his help last night and his hospitality this morning." I made eye contact with Rook. He gave me a slight nod, and I gave him a hug from the front this time.

"Be careful not to harm any petals," Dorian warned mockingly. "Rook isn't known for being a gentle giant."

I walked by Dorian and stopped when we were shoulder to shoulder, facing opposite directions. "Maybe this flower likes it a little rough." I looked back at Rook and winked. He inhaled deeply as he looked me up and down before meeting my eyes with hunger. I said that just to pester Dorian, but with Rook looking at me like that, I was totally on board with whatever was going through his mind. I was willing to try almost anything once.

* * *

Ledger sat in the backseat of Jem's truck, sandwiched between Gia and Julie. Clara sat in front, staring dreamily at Jem.

"You're welcome to sit on my lap, gorgeous?" Ledger wiggled his eyebrows and patted his thigh.

"I have a middle seat up here, Lyss." Jem jumped out so I could slide into the seat between him and Clara.

The ride home was pretty relaxed. Clara gave directions to Jem, Ledger entertained Julie and Gia in the back, I just watched the scenery.

Jem pulled up in front of our apartment complex. The four of us had been roommates since college and kept the tradition going after we graduated last year. Plus rent was expensive, so it was the more practical solution.

"Lyss, can I talk to you for a second?"

I paused halfway out the door at Jem's request. I waved to the girls, letting them know I'd be a minute before pulling my leg back into the truck and turning to face Jem. Ledger leaned against the door to wait for me to get out.

"What's up?" I asked.

"You may have heard that the band is taking a year's hiatus," he began.

I shook my head, unsure of why he was bringing this up.

"The party was to celebrate our last concert before we take some time off. What are your thoughts on that?"

My mouth opened, then closed. "Um, that's good, I guess?"

Jem ran his hand through his hair. "I'm not asking correctly. As a social media manager, what are your thoughts on that? Will we lose the momentum we've gained up here? In the music industry, I mean."

Okay, now that made more sense. "I have no experience in the music industry, but from an advertising standpoint, unless you have something huge planned for a year from now that you're promoting and keeping you on people's minds, then yeah, you'll probably run out of steam." I wasn't going to lie, but the truth hurt sometimes. "You'll still have your hardcore fans, I don't think you'll ever lose

Clara or Gia, but your music will slowly be played less often on the radio, there will be less talk about you since there will be nothing new to talk about."

Jem nodded. "That's what I thought."

"Jem, quit being such a wimp and just ask her." Ledger grabbed my shoulders and pulled me backwards. I shrieked as I started falling out of the truck, but Ledger caught me with one hand behind my head and one wrapped around my waist. "Beautiful, talented Lyss. Will you do us the honor of becoming our social media manager?"

I burst out laughing. My bottom half was still in the truck, but my top half was two seconds away from a free fall to the ground, so I held onto Ledger's biceps. His large, muscular biceps.

"Don't you guys have a PR company or something that handles that?" I asked.

"We used to, but we fired him after we found out that he would message fans as us. He would make it seem like one of us wanted to date them, then when they agreed to meet, he would be the hero to swoop in when we didn't show up for whatever reason," Jem said.

"Yeah, the last girl I was 'messaging' got told I had an STD." Ledger frowned and tensed his arms. I squeezed appreciatively, and his frown quickly turned into a smile.

"Why me though? You don't even know me. For all you know, I could totally suck."

"Promises, promises," Ledger muttered as he leaned down to snuggle into my neck. I giggled at his tickling nose and smacked his arm.

"Sit her back up, Ledge, she's not going to be able to think with all the blood going to her head."

"All the blood is going to my head too," Ledger said.

I rolled my eyes, earning a laugh from him as he lifted me back into the truck.

"Enough of your pathetic pickup lines," Jem told Ledger.

"Pathetic? I think you mean incredibly witty. Right, Lyss?"

I held up my hands. "I'm not getting in the middle of you two."

"But you already are," Ledger whispered into my ear, pressing his chest against my back. I shivered at the double entendre and my mind went from simply sitting between the two handsome men, to being pressed between these two while naked. Damn Ledger St. James and his sex appeal.

"Here's the deal," Jem said. "I was going to take over our social media because I figured it couldn't be that hard. But when you explained to me everything you do, I realized that I'm way out of my current." His eyes pleaded with me. "We want someone who knows us and will post behind-the-scenes type of stuff, because, as you mentioned, the mysterious thing is only going to last for so long."

"But I don't know you," I protested. "Clara and Gia are the big fans that can quote your birthdays, likes and dislikes, who Ledger has dated, which gyms Rook likes to frequent. At best, I can sing along with a couple of your songs." And think you're all hot as hell, but I wasn't going to mention that part.

"That's exactly why we want you. We want someone that sees us as people. You didn't fall at Dorian's feet. Rook doesn't intimidate you. Ledger's come-ons don't seem to affect you."

"Give it time. I'm like water dripping onto a rock. I'll get through, eventually." Ledger twirled a piece of my hair around his finger.

Jem and I ignored him and continued our conversation.

"That actually makes sense." I chewed on my thumbnail as I thought. "What social media platforms are you wanting me to cover?"

"Just the main ones." He named several of the most popular platforms, all ones that I was comfortable with.

"Are you wanting content or for me to handle comments and replies as well?"

"Comments and replies as well. We want our fans to feel like there's actually someone there. We try to get on when we can, but we can't keep up with it without going crazy. We looked you up and found some of the accounts you manage. They're organized, professional, but still fun."

"How much time are you expecting from me? Ten hours a week? Twenty?"

Jem looked over my shoulder at Ledger with a concerned look. "Um, that's where we've run into some problems. Along with managing our social media, we want someone that actually knows us and can show more behind the scenes."

"Yeah, you mentioned that." I looked behind me at Ledger curiously. What were these guys wanting?

"You're swimming around the point again, and not in the fun way," Ledger said. He pulled me back once more, so I was halfway in his arms again. "Gorgeous, fearless Lyss. We want you to move in with us."

My eyes popped open wide. "Move in with you?" I squeaked.

"The more you're around us, the quicker you'll get to know us and the easier it will be for you to do your job. And it will be easier for us to open up to you the more comfortable we are around you," Jem explained.

"There's no way Dorian agreed to this," I said, shaking my head.

"He was outvoted," Ledger said.

"But he didn't exactly vote against it," Jem added.

I chewed on my thumbnail again, trusting Ledger to not drop me if I didn't have two hands holding onto him. "I can't just ditch the girls. Even with the four of us paying rent, it's still not cheap. And I still have other clients and waitress part-time."

"You can still pay rent here. Room and board with us will be included with us and we'll pay you weekly." Jem named off a number that had my jaw dropping. It was more than twice what I was currently making with my current clients and at my part-time waitressing job.

"How long are you wanting to use me?"

Ledger scrunched up his nose. "'Use me' sounds so dirty, don't you think? We don't want to use you, Lyss. Use us to build up your portfolio, but we just want your help, however much you're willing to give."

That was so sweet, especially coming from Ledger.

"I guess I could quit my waitressing job, but I'm not dropping my other social media clients."

"That's fine. We don't expect you to drop everything for us. Like Ledger said, we just want whatever help you're willing to give us. We'll agree to pay for a minimum of six months, but if, at any time, you don't feel comfortable, you can quit."

I thought quietly for a moment. If I kept my current clients, I would still have that steady income. Getting a job as a waitress would be easy enough when the boys were done with my services. Ugh, Ledger was right. That sounded dirty. I'd still be able to pay my part of rent, plus add some cushion to my savings. For rock stars, the boys were all pretty nice. Except Dorian, but there was always one, right? I liked Jem's sweet shyness and honesty. I enjoyed Ledger's cheesy pickup lines and the way he made me laugh. Rook's quiet strength made me feel safe and comfortable, even if I knew he could probably snap my neck with two fingers.

"I can quit anytime I feel uncomfortable? No questions asked?"

"Anytime. We want your help, not be your keepers," Jem said.

"Can I take the day to think about it?"

Ledger whooped and kissed me right on the mouth before pushing me back in the cab. "She said yes!" He held his hands above his head and ran a lap around the truck.

I laughed at his theatrics, and Jem just shook his head.

"She said she'd think about it," Jem said as Ledger ran past his window.

"When would you want me to start?" I asked.

"I can have the papers drawn up and ready to go as soon as Monday." He pushed back his red-streaked hair and looked at me hopefully.

Whoa, they weren't messing around. "I would need at least two weeks. I'd have to put in my notice at work and pack." I frowned as I mentally began a list of other things I would need to do.

Jem nodded. "Let me give you my number. You can text or call me with any other questions and let me know when you've made your decision."

I handed him my phone to enter his information.

"See you later, doll," Ledger said when I climbed out of the truck.

I waved goodbye to the boys and went to my apartment to tell the girls.

Chapter 6

Lyss

As I expected, the girls had been spying on me from our apartment window and pounced on me as soon as I came in.

"What did they want?" Gia asked.

"Did you almost fall out of the truck?" Julie questioned.

"Did Ledger actually kiss you?" That was from Clara.

I sat down on our sofa and they all gathered around, waiting for my answers.

"They asked me to move in with them," I said slowly, still trying to process the conversation I just had with Jem and Ledger.

Gia looked confused, Clara started laughing, and Julie just stared at me.

Clara's laughter died down when I said nothing else. "Say what now?"

"They want me to be their social media manager," I said.

"Why would you have to move in with them to do that? You have other clients and you don't live with them." Gia still looked concerned.

They all, unsurprisingly, knew about *Sons of Poseidon* taking a year off. I told them how Jem had asked about how that would affect their fan base and what I told him. Then I told them what he had proposed and the amount that was offered.

Clara flopped onto the floor and moaned about not being the favored one of the gods and goddesses of hunky men.

"What are you going to do?" Gia asked as she ignored Clara's dramatics.

"She's going to say yes." Julie looked at me expectantly.

"I don't know." I covered my face with my hands.

"I think Julie's right," Gia said.

I peeked through my fingers and parroted Clara's earlier phrase. "Say what now?"

"The guys seem nice enough," Gia said.

"Except Dorian," I mumbled.

"What do you have against Dorian? He was just as welcoming as the others," Julie said. "Rook's the only one that makes me a little nervous, but that's because I didn't see him smile once and he has such an intense stare."

I shrugged. Rook didn't intimidate me in the slightest.

"Dorian was a total douche. Did you hear how he kept calling me Amaryllis?"

Gia winced. She knew how much I hated my full name.

"Boo-hoo, one of the sexy, ripped, drool-worthy rock stars isn't under your spell," Clara said from the floor.

I very maturely stuck my tongue out at her and looked at Gia. "You really think I should do it?"

"Hell yeah. You can focus on your dream job full time, add some fantastic references to your resume, and spend time with guys that are both hot and sweet? How are you even questioning this?" Gia tapped me on the forehead with her palm.

"When you put it that way," I grumbled.

"They said you can quit if you don't feel like it's working. We're still in the same town so you can come over for girls' night," Julie added.

"Or we can go over there!" Clara sat up with a huge smile.

"I think it's settled," Gia said. "You're going to call up Jem and tell him you would be thrilled to work with *Sons of Poseidon*."

* * *

I called Jem a couple of hours later—I didn't want to seem too eager—and let him know I would take the position. I heard Ledger whooping in the background again and grinned. At least I knew some of them would be glad to have me there. Jem said he'd have paperwork drawn up and ready to look over when I moved in.

The next two weeks went by quickly. I put in my two weeks at the restaurant I worked at. The boss wished me luck and told me I could come back if I ever needed to and they even threw me a little going away party. It was leftover cake that was going to get tossed that evening, but it was the thought that counted.

Back at home, I packed up my stuff, stood in my room and looked around. Most of my clothes were in suitcases, and I had a box of decor and personal items. Since I wasn't one-hundred percent sure how this was going to work out, I didn't want to move everything, and I knew I could always come back to get what I needed.

I was full of nervous energy the day I was leaving. I could have left in the morning, but I wanted to see Gia, Julie, and Clara before I left. We wouldn't be too far away, but it was still going to be different than living together. And it sounded like I was going to be busy.

Since I still had a few hours to spare, I worked on social media for my other clients, responding to questions, scheduling posts, and emailing updates. I puttered around the apartment, tidying up to burn off nervous energy.

What was I thinking moving in with four guys that I barely knew? Even after an intensive web search, I hadn't learned that much about them. Their roles in the band, birthdays, favorite food, which is sushi for all of them. But there was no mention of hometowns, parents, siblings, how the band got together. It was like they just appeared one day.

I could see why they needed a social media manager, but why did they suddenly want to open up to the world? Probably for sales. Isn't that the driving force of the industry?

My phone chimed, notifying me I had a text message. It was from a number that I didn't recognize.

UNKNOWN

Hey, doll, what time are you coming over?

I smiled and text back.

LYSS

Hey Ledger. I'll be there around six-thirty. I wanted to say goodbye to the girls before I left.

LEDGER

How did you know it was me?

LYSS

You're the only one that calls me "doll." Probably because you call every girl that so you don't have to remember our names. ;)

LEDGER

Ha, that's what you think. I call all the other girls babe. I only call you doll because of your big doll eyes.

That surprised me. And made me feel a little special. If what he was saying was true and not just another line.

LYSS

You're also the biggest flirt I've ever met, so I knew it had to be you.

LEDGER

Aw, you can even recognize my charm over text! We're just meant to be.

I laughed and shook my head at his antics. Life would be entertaining living with them.

LYSS

See you later this evening.

LEDGER

I'm counting the minutes.

I put my phone down after programming Ledger's number into my phone. If he wasn't so funny and charming, his lame pickup lines would be beyond ridiculous and cringy.

Knowing the girls would be home around five, I threw together the quick dinner of spaghetti and garlic bread I had planned. They all came in and breathed deeply through their noses, inhaling the simmering scents of the marinara. Clara was the last one to arrive, and we all sat down to eat. When we finished, they helped me load up my turquoise Jeep Rubicon. We hugged each other like I was moving across the country, not forty-five minutes away.

"If they do anything that they're not supposed to, you call me and I'll come over and whoop their asses," Julie said.

I laughed as I hugged her. Those creeps may have gotten the best of her, almost, at the party, but in full form, Julie was scrappy and not afraid to stand up for the ones she loved.

"Send me as many pictures of Jem shirtless as you can," Clara requested. "Hell, I'll take pictures of any of them in any state of undress."

Gia was the last one to hug me. "Don't let them push you around. You're a strong woman. Don't let a man let you lose sight of that."

I hugged her extra tightly. "I feel like I'm moving across the country, not just across town."

"We're here for you if you need us, but make sure you have fun. All work and no play."

"Makes a girl a bad lay," I finished.

I waved goodbye as I drove away, the address Jem sent me programmed into my GPS. If I did well with this assignment, maybe

I could start pulling other high-profile clients. I could even start hiring people to work under me so that I had more free time. This could end up working out really well. Plus, I would get to know some really cute guys that were already affecting me with their unique personalities.

Bright blue eyes with dark furrowed brows over them flashed through my mind. Or this could go really bad and I could end up on the front page as the employee that throat-punched her rock star boss one day.

* * *

I pulled into the long driveway three minutes after six-thirty. Ledger bounded out of the house, followed closely by Jem and Rook. As soon as I stepped out of my jeep, Ledger wrapped me up in a hug and spun me in a circle. I squealed and held on tightly to his neck.

"You find the place okay?" Jem asked.

"Not a problem. It's like the GPS knew exactly where I wanted to go," I teased.

Ledger laughed and wrapped an arm around my shoulders.

"Is this all you have?" Rook asked.

I turned around and saw that he was already unloading my luggage. "Yeah, I wasn't sure what I would need or—" I cut myself off, not wanting to voice my fears of not being able to hack it in front of the guys.

"If things would work out here?" Jem suggested.

I shrugged my shoulders and gave him a guilty nod.

"Don't worry, doll, you're going to love it here." Ledger grabbed my hand and pulled me inside, leaving Rook and Jem following behind with my luggage.

Ledger walked straight to the room that the girls were staying in before. Instead of the boring tan and cream I remember from before, it was full of pops of color. The walls were a pale shade of aqua, making it feel like we were outside on a cloud free day. Gauzy white curtains blew gently from the breeze the open balcony door was letting in. The bed was covered in a white and coral comforter with bright aqua pillows covering it. A lamp sat on the nightstand, a mama and baby turtle shaping the lamp's body. Old looking netting decorated the wall above the bed with shells and starfish placed throughout.

"Is it okay?" Jem asked. "We wanted you to feel at home here, so we had someone come in and decorate it."

"I love it." I jumped up and landed on my back on the bed. It dipped to my right side, and I rolled right into Ledger's arms.

"And plenty big enough for two," he said while wrapping his arms around me.

I pushed at his chest, and he let go of me easily.

"Okay, we need a few ground rules if this is going to work," I said.

Ledger groaned but got up and went to stand with Rook and Jem.

I groaned too, but for an entirely different reason. "Maybe it would be best to do this as a full group." Meaning we needed Dorian here.

"Let's move into the kitchen," Jem suggested before I could figure out a way to say that in no way did I want Dorian in my room. Even if it was technically their room and I was just using it. "I have the contract ready to sign, as long as you find it satisfactory."

"I'll get Dorian," Rook grumbled.

"Need some backup?" Ledger clasped Rook's shoulder and walked down the hall with him.

Rook growled and pushed Ledger into the wall. Ledger just laughed it off and came back to join me and Jem. The three of us made our way to the kitchen to sit at the table and wait for Rook and Dorian.

Dorian was sweaty and shirtless when he came in and my mouth dried up. I tried to ignore him, but failed miserably with his bare chest on display.

"I hear Amaryllis has to lay down some rules in *our* house." He walked to the cupboard to grab a cup and filled it from the fridge.

"Going up the stairs a little exhausting for you, Dory?" I asked.

He smirked. "I was working out, if you must know. But please, feel free to continue ogling the goods."

I tilted my head to the side. "Gladly. Rook, would you be a dear and take off your shirt?"

Rook, Ledger, and Jem all burst out laughing while Dorian scowled. He took a seat at the table without any more wise cracks and glared at me.

"Alright, Amaryllis, your audience is here. What do you want?" Dorian asked.

"First, I want to know exactly what you guys expect from me. Jem gave me enough of the rundown to convince me to accept this job, but I'd like to hear from the rest of you." I clasped my hands together and set them on the table in front of me.

"Jem is probably the best one to tell you. He's all organized and shit like that," Ledger said.

Jem opened the manila folder he had sitting in front of him and handed me a stack of papers. "Here's what we're looking for from you, the green sticky note marks where it states what you can expect from us."

We spent the next half hour reading through it together and making sure we were all on the same page, no pun intended. It was basically what Jem had already told me. They wanted me to get to know them and see what their life was like and relay that to the fans. I would create the content, including occasionally taking the pictures, schedule it, reply to comments, and keep the drama in the comments down to a minimum. From them, I would get free room and board, a very nice weekly paycheck, and all expenses paid if I had to go with them on a trip. It was impossible to turn down.

"If everything meets your mighty expectations, some of us have things to do," Dorian said.

"Just a couple more things," I said. "I get two days off a week. I still need to provide for my other clients at full capacity, and regardless of what you might think, us lowly people have lives, too."

"That's one." Dorian linked his fingers, placed them behind his head, and leaned back in his chair. I hated the way it emphasized his broad chest. "What's the other thing?"

"My room is my space. No coming in unless I've given permission. I realize this is your house, but if room and board are part of my pay, that makes the room mine."

"Don't worry, Amaryllis, no one is going to sneak in and have their wicked way with you in the middle of the night."

"There go my plans," Ledger mourned.

"There are plenty of women that are more than willing to climb in our beds and suck our dicks. No need to scare us from forcing your frigid legs open." Dorian got up and started walking away while I ground my teeth together.

"Just a minute!" I hit the table with the palm of my hand as I stood up. I marched to Dorian and jabbed my finger in his chest. "What the hell is your problem with me?"

"You mean aside from your lovely first impression?" he drawled.

"I apologized for spilling the drink on you. Haven't you ever heard of accidents?"

"I meant the one where you insisted on calling me Dory after I explained what my name was."

"You started it," I said. "You called me Amaryllis."

Dorian laughed. "There's that childish side showing again."

"If my childish side was showing, I would have punched you in the dick by now."

"No need to make up lame excuses to touch my dick. If you ask really nicely, I might just let you have the honor of seeing it."

My jaw dropped. "You're a pig."

"And you're annoying me right now." He did an about face and headed out of the room, but I couldn't let him have the last word.

"Third thing," I called out. "You have to stop being such an asshole to me."

"Or what?" he laughed and kept walking.

"I'll tell everyone that you're impotent."

That stopped him. He turned around slowly. "No one would believe you."

"Wouldn't they though? The girl who's living with *Sons of Poseidon*? I could talk to all the girls you sleep with, or rather, attempt to sleep with. Maybe you pay them off just to say you rocked their world." My finger tapped on my chin. "I could even be a firsthand account. Think of all the ways I could come up with about how the grumpy lead singer swept me off my feet. I could build it up for weeks, making it look like we've gone on fancy dates, how I'm falling in love with you. Then just when things are about to peak..." I looked down at Dorian's shorts, then back up to his face with a pouty look. "They deflate. It's okay, it happens to a lot of people. They even make pills for it."

If steam had started coming out of Dorian's ears, I wouldn't have been shocked.

"Don't mess with a girl who writes for a living," I warned him. "We can come up with all kinds of ways to make you pay."

I waved to the other three guys, who were looking at me with varying looks of impressed, shocked, and nervous, and glided back to my room. Might as well unpack and get settled in.

Chapter 7

Ledger

Holy shit, our girl could hold her own. Pretty much everyone who met Dorian, whether here or back home, practically bowed and scraped to make the guy happy. Rook, Jem, and I were the few exceptions. And now Lyss. I loved watching her hand Dorian's ass to him.

Dorian began spending a lot of extra time in the gym once Lyss moved in. Every time they were in the same room, he couldn't help making some sort of comment to piss her off. Lyss gave as good as she got, though, and it was a thing of beauty to watch her. Maybe I was twisted, but I loved seeing her cheeks turn pink as she looked down her nose at Dorian, even though she only reached his chin.

I got her to blush as often as I could, not the way Dorian did, though. No, I had my own ways, my favorite being putting on some music and dancing with her around the room. She always laughed and pretended she didn't want to, but I could tell she loved it by the way her eyes sparkled and how she could never stop smiling.

As much as I wanted to work my magic and get her into my bed, I knew what Jem had said was right. We didn't want to scare her away with all of us pursuing her at once. Jem, Rook, and even Dorian, since

Jem had pointed it out, liked Lyss. And how could we not? She treated us like people. There were no stars in her eyes when she looked at us. No trying to get us alone just so she could say she slept with a rock star. No ulterior motives of using us for our status to raise their status.

She made amazing omelets. She looked great in a bikini, which she wore often since we all loved being in the water and hung out in and around the pool often. Sometimes, she was content to sit in silence. No need to fill it with inane chatter like a lot of other girls. Her nose scrunched up in the cutest way when she was trying not to laugh.

Jem bonded with her over books. Her favorites were romances while Jem's were action and horror, but they still found plenty to talk about. Jem was used to being in the background with Dorian as a cousin. It was good to see him taking the lead finally.

She had no fear of Rook, which wasn't something we often saw. Even the girls he slept with usually ran off as soon as the deed was done. And he had a total soft spot for her.

And even though he wouldn't admit, Dorian loved the way she stood up to him and pushed right back.

Yeah, she had us all wrapped around her little finger.

Dorian, Jem, and I were out for a swim tonight while Rook stayed back with Lyss. I would love to volunteer to be the one to stay with her every time and have the extra one-on-one time, but even a beautiful woman couldn't hold me back from the call of the sea.

"It's been nice having Lyss here," Jem said.

Dorian grunted and rolled his eyes, but didn't say anything.

"It has," I agreed with Jem. Partly because I did agree, and partly to annoy Dorian. The guy needed to be reminded he wasn't a god occasionally, and I'd taken on the responsibility to do that for years.

"I knew she would fit in, but I'm still surprised how well she does. It's only been a couple weeks, and it feels like she's been here forever."

I rolled onto my back to swim alongside him. "She even has Rook whipped."

"I like her."

"Duh, we all do," I said.

Jem looked at me now. "No, I really like her."

I nodded my head. I knew exactly what he meant and how he felt, because I did too.

"We can't let her get between us. If she chooses someone, we can't let it ruin us," Jem said. His brow furrowed as he ran different scenarios through his head. He had always been the quiet thinker in the background. Some people made fun of him for it, but his brain helped us get to where we're at.

"So if she chooses me, you'll be fine with it?" I already knew his answer, but I couldn't resist ribbing him a little.

"If you're who she wants, then, yes." Jem said the words, but his face told another story.

"You guys are making a big deal over some tail," Dorian said.

"Don't think we haven't noticed you checking out her ass when she puts something in the oven or try pissing her off just so she'll talk to you," I said.

Dorian flipped me the bird then dove under the water to swim away from us.

"Maybe she doesn't have to choose," I drawled. Our attraction to her wasn't one-sided. If she wanted more than just one of us, who was I to stand in the way of love?

"What do you mean?" Jem looked at me curiously. Where he was the thinker, I was the one with the crazy ideas. Someone had to lighten these guys up a bit.

"We all like her, and I know she likes all of us, even grumpy Dorian." I shrugged. "And it's not like we haven't shared before."

"You guys have, I haven't. And it's been for sex. One night and they're gone. I don't want just one night with Lyss."

"I don't think one night would be enough with her," I said.

Honestly, I think just one night would make it worse than not having her at all. "But, I'm not just talking about sex."

We swam together in silence as I waited for Jem to process my subtle suggestion.

"How would it work?" he asked finally. "Would it be like an open relationship?"

"Not open exactly. I'm okay sharing her with you guys, but if anyone else comes near her, I'll kill them." My jaw clenched at the thought of someone else making her smile, touching her, feeling her.

Jem rubbed his chin. "I think I could be okay with that. The problem is, even if we're all on board for that, what makes you think she would be?"

"We simply have to convince her."

"And how do we go about doing that?"

I grinned. "Jem, my little understudy, we just have to make her realize she can't settle for just one of us."

Chapter 8

Lyss

The first couple of weeks were spent by the pool. My idea of a good time is relaxing with a good book, but when there were three ripped men lounging with me or swimming laps, it was almost a dream. Dorian spent most of his time inside doing who knew what. The times he came out, he did his best to ignore me. Fine by me, I wasn't going to deal with the asshole when I had Jem to discuss my favorite books and TV shows with, Ledger using me as his personal guinea pig for non-alcoholic drinks he came up with, or Rook to indulge my love of cooking with while we made dinner together. Not to mention the heated stares I got from each of them, especially when we were by the pool.

There was never inappropriate touching, but there were plenty of touches that fueled inappropriate thoughts. Hands on my waist when Ledger pretended to throw me in the pool. Shoulders rubbing when Jem and I shared passages in books we were reading. Bodies brushing against each other when Rook and I shared the kitchen.

How much could a girl take before she combusted? I thought it would be easy to view them as clients and be professional, even if the setting wasn't a traditional one. That was definitely wishful, and stupid, thinking on my part. I was just glad I had remembered to bring my little nightstand toy. It was definitely getting quite the workout lately.

The first outing we had with me as the official social media manager was an interview with a local radio station. We all rode together in Dorian's SUV. Rook and Ledger sandwiched me between them while Jem rode shotgun and Dorian drove with a stony look on his face. The three of us in the back talked and joked, and the other two stayed quiet.

When we got to the radio station, Dorian pulled up to the front to an area blocked off for us to go in. There were a decent amount of fans there. Some were holding home made posters saying which member of the band they loved. Some were glued to their phones while they recorded their close encounter. Some were thrusting pens out for the guys to grab. One girl whipped her shirt off and screamed for them to sign her boobs.

The guys handled it well. They signed a couple autographs, all on paper though, no boobs, smiled for pictures, said hi. I hung back to give the guys space and take video. I could get still shots from it later for pictures and post snippets of the video on different platforms. I followed behind them until Rook placed his hand on my lower back and ushered me forward through the doors.

He let out a breath when the doors closed behind us, muffling the noise from the crowd.

"You okay?" I asked him quietly.

He nodded. "I'm used to it, but I still don't like the whole adoring fan thing. It's kind of weird."

"Aren't adoring fans one reason you became a musician?" I tilted my head and smiled up at him so he knew I was teasing.

"There were other factors at play," he said.

Rook's mysterious answer had me frowning until Ledger caught up with us.

"Unlike Rook, I'm all for the screaming girls."

"I know all about your reputation with girls," I said.

65

"Don't be jealous, doll. My eyes are only for you now."

I rolled my eyes and laughed. "Until a cute girl with a big ass or boobs screams your name."

Ledger leaned in close until I could feel his breath on my ear. "The only girl I want screaming my name is you. And I want to be the one making you scream it," he said.

My cheeks burned at the thought and my body wasn't opposed to the idea if my nipples hardening meant anything. Ledger shot me a knowing look and walked ahead to the front of the group.

An assistant met up with us and led the way to the studio. There was a table in the room and several microphones lined up next to each other. A man was sitting at the other end wearing headphones and tapping away on his computer. He was handsome with a wide smile, sun-kissed hair, and blue eyes. A white polo accentuated his tan and pulled his all-American boy look together.

"Hey, guys, good to meet you, I'm Rob." He stood up and walked around the table to shake hands with the guys.

I found a chair in a corner of the room and sat quietly, pulling out my phone to snap a few pictures to post later. A large hand appeared in front of my face while I started taking screenshots from the video. I looked up to see Rob smiling down at me.

"I'm going to go out on a limb and say you're not the newest member of the *Sons of Poseidon*."

I put my hand in his to shake it and smiled back. "Nope, I'm just Lyss, the social media manager."

"There is no 'just' about you, Lyss. And I'm glad to hear you're the social media manager. I was worried you were a girlfriend to one of these guys."

"I just met them a couple of weeks ago. Definitely not a girlfriend."

There was a tap on the window surrounding the studio and someone held up two fingers on the other side.

"Show's about to start, but hopefully we can talk after?" He looked at me hopefully.

I nodded. "That sounds great."

Rob's grin brightened, and he went back to his seat. When I looked at the guys, Rook and Ledger were looking at Rob through narrow eyes while Jem maintained a blank expression. Meanwhile, Dorian glared at me like I had done something wrong. I glared back before focusing on my phone so I could ignore him.

After welcoming listeners back to the show, Rob introduced the guys. "I promised you all a special guest and I may have lied, because we actually have four. Let's welcome the *Sons of Poseidon* to the studio!" Rob hit a button on his laptop and cheers sounded. "You guys just finished up your latest tour. Every venue was sold out, which is amazing. Why are you taking a break just when things are getting good?"

"It really was quite amazing to play in front of so many people at each performance. We can't thank our fans enough for their support and their love," Jem said. "We have some personal things coming up that we need to focus on. During that time, we'll also be working on some new songs, and get things planned for when we come back."

"I'm sure it's safe for me to say that everyone listening right now will keep their ears wide open for that announcement. Now let's get to the good stuff. I already have a list of questions from listeners coming in. We'll start things off with Shannon. She wants to ask Ledger what superpower he would choose if he could."

"Shape shifting," Ledger answered. The other guys all tried to hold back their snickers and failed.

"That was a quick answer. I'm guessing you've given this some thought before?" Rob asked.

"Once or twice." Ledger lifted a shoulder lazily.

"Next one is for Rook. What is the most ridiculous thing anyone has ever tricked you into doing?" Rob turned his attention to Rook.

"Joining a band."

Rob laughed until he saw Rook didn't even crack a smile. "Alright, let's go to Dorian. Do you sing in the shower?"

"Who doesn't?" Dorian held his hands up guiltily. "To be honest, it's one of the best places to test out new songs. You're relaxed, alone, the acoustics are great." Dorian turned his head to look directly at me. "I do some of my best work in the shower."

My breath caught. I had been taking another video, but I stopped it and put my hands in my lap. The look he gave me made me picture him in the shower. I already knew what his bare torso looked like. There was a pool in the backyard that they all took advantage of often and wet swim trunks sometimes clung to the body. I zoned out for a minute, thinking about that, only brought back when I caught Dorian's smirk. He knew exactly what was going through my head. I glared at him before I turned my head and looked at anything else but him.

The guys answered some more questions, taking a couple of commercial breaks in between. During one break, an assistant came in with water bottles for everyone, including me.

"What do you think so far?" Rob got up from his seat and came to stand by me.

"It's interesting. Do you get to interview different bands and artists often?"

He shrugged. "A couple of times a month. Sometimes it's just phone interviews. Those aren't as much fun because you can't really see who you're talking to. It can get lonely in the studio sometimes."

"Well, you seem like a natural at it."

"Thanks." He smiled and leaned against the wall. "So what's it like being the social media manager for such a popular band? What do you do exactly?"

"I can't really say what it's like since I haven't been working with them long, but so far it's been fun. They're a talented group of guys. Basically, I'm just here to take videos and pictures and give a more behind-the-scenes look at them."

"That sounds even more exciting than my job. Did you want to grab some coffee after this? I'll be off when the interview is over."

"Oh, um, I'm not sure. I drove with the guys so I'd—"

There was a knock at the window again.

"Think about it and we can talk after," Rob said. I nodded in agreement, and he rushed back to his seat.

The light in the studio turned on again to signal that they were back on the air. Rob welcomed everyone back and did a quick recap of what they were doing.

I took more video of the interview and wrote down little bits of information the guys shared so I could remember them. The interview didn't last much longer and soon Rob signed off and the guys all stood up. I waited while they shook hands and Rob thanked them again for taking the time to come to the studio before coming to talk to me.

"So, what do you think? Coffee?" He looked at me hopefully.

I hadn't given it a lot of thought since I was working during the last part of the interview, but he was nice, handsome, and had a job. I opened my mouth to agree, but Dorian stood next to me and answered for me.

"She doesn't drink coffee."

Rob looked at Dorian as if wondering where he had come from. "That's fine. They serve other things. Tea, smoothies, water. We can even go somewhere else if you want." Rob looked at me as he said the last part.

"She's busy." Dorian took my wrist and pulled me towards the door. "Let's go, Amaryllis."

I bristled at his use of my name.

"How about we let her answer?" Rob grabbed Dorian's wrist.

Dorian stared at his hand before slowly raising his gaze to his. Rob slowly let go and looked at me.

"Lyss, are you okay?" Rob asked quietly.

I shook Dorian's hand off of me and glared at him before turning my attention to Rob.

"I'm fine. Some people are just overly touchy with their toys, one of which I have to keep reminding him I am not." I glared at Dorian again. "Thanks for the offer, Rob, but I think it's best if I just head home. I still have a bunch of work to do."

Rob looked at the ground and nodded before pasting a smile back on. "Sure. If you change your mind or need to get a hold of me, just call the station."

"I will. Thanks." I shot him a smile before brushing past Dorian to where the other three guys were waiting outside the door.

The guys boxed me in, whether it was conscious or not, I wasn't sure. Dorian stood to my right, Jem stood to my left, Ledger behind me, and Rook in front. When we walked outside, we all went straight to the car. The guys smiled and waved, reminding of those crazy penguins from Madagascar, but didn't bother stopping to sign any autographs or take pictures.

Rook opened the back door and Jem got in. Dorian pushed me into the car and followed. The door slammed shut behind him. Ledger got into the front seat and Rook slid into the driver's seat.

When we drove away, I whirled on Dorian. "What the hell, Dory?"

Dorian looked at me with a slight lift of his brow. "What?"

"What? You're seriously going to play dumb with me right now?" My hands clenched into fists where they sat on my lap. "You cock blocked me."

"Such language, Amaryllis." Dorian tutted. "If you want cock, there's plenty in here that I'm sure could satisfy you."

He did not just say that. My neck and cheeks warmed until I could feel them burning.

"I wouldn't want your cock even if you handed it to me on a platter."

"I didn't mean mine, but then I didn't know you were so eager for it. I could always use a quick fuck to take off the edge before I find something more entertaining."

This must be how a teapot felt as the water inside was slowly heated and pressure built. I let out a shriek of frustration loud enough to make Dorian wince and unbuckled my seatbelt.

"Right now? It might make the other guys jealous, but I'm okay with that." Dorian's smile was cocky. He spread his legs wider and sunk down in his seat, getting into position.

I turned around and kneeled on the seat before crawling into the third row head first. The heel of my shoe hit something and Dorian grunted.

"Oops," I said with zero apology in my voice when I made it to the back. I buckled myself into the seat and stretched my arms out along the back of the seat.

"Hey, Ledger. Put some music on," I called up front.

"Yes, ma'am." A snicker followed his response.

The radio turned on and one of their songs was blasting through the speakers with Dorian's voice singing the lyrics.

"Something less whiny," I said.

Jem snorted a laugh and changed the station. Taylor Swift crooned about living in a city.

"Much better," I said.

Rook, Ledger, and Jem all laughed then. Dorian was still gazing out the window, but I could see the tension in his shoulders. Take that, asshole.

Chapter 9

Lyss

The next couple of months seemed to fly by. Most of our days were spent just hanging out with occasional appearances sprinkled in. Thankfully, nothing as embarrassing or frustrating as our first one at the radio station. Mostly just meet and greets and a couple more local interviews. The band manager for the *Sons of Poseidon* was trying to get them to set a date for another tour, but the guys kept pushing it off.

The guys had an unhealthy obsession with sushi and I learned more about it with them than I ever had before. I was not a raw fish kind of girl. They always ordered a few rolls of tempura style for me, just like they always tried to get me to try new flavors. I could stomach a few bites of the maki or uramaki rolls as long as the fish-to-other-ingredient ratio was low, but the nigirii still made me gag.

Rook was the unofficial cook of the group for the meals they didn't order out. Something I never would have expected from the tattooed man with biceps the size of my head. I started helping in the mornings, flipping pancakes while he scrambled eggs and cooked the bacon and sausages. Sometimes, I would make omelets and he would make biscuits from scratch that were fluffier than a Pomeranian's tail.

We took turns planning dinner for the nights we didn't get takeout, and it became our little thing.

He also took it on himself to be the buffer between me and Dorian. The big guy had my back, and it confused Dorian to no end.

* * *

"Get me some more French toast, Amaryllis," Dorian demanded one morning after he had finished the one on his plate.

Before I could snark out a comment about hell freezing over, Rook spoke up.

"Don't speak to her like that. She's not here to feed you or serve you. Unless you want her to post a picture of how cute you think your breakfast is on Instagram or to tell her thank you for the meal, don't talk to her about your food. You can get your own damn French toast." He neatly cut a piece of the egg battered bread and put it into his mouth while I stared at him in shock. I was used to the guys letting me hold my own, but to hear Rook basically tell him to piss off was a thing of beauty.

Ledger got up to refill his coffee and cover up his laughter. Jem looked at me, equally amused. I peeked over at Dorian. He was still in shock that Rook had spoken to him that way. He caught me looking, and I stuck my tongue out at him. Not my most mature moment, but I couldn't help it. He growled and pushed back, knocking his chair over, and stomped off to his bedroom.

* * *

Ledger was the one who was always up for anything whether it was running to the store for a forgotten ingredient for me, a late night dip in the ocean with Rook, singing lyrics while Jem played when writing a new song, or even putting up with Dorian's surly attitude in the gym downstairs. One morning, he grabbed me and twirled me around the living room, singing Beautiful, Crazy by Toby Keith. I never knew what to expect from him, aside from his smile and endless positivity. He was also the fitness guru of the group and made sure everyone was getting their workouts in. I tried to avoid him as much as possible during those times, but he always found me and made me come work out with him after the other guys were done.

* * *

"Come on, Lyss. You can do one more."

We were doing pull-ups today. When I first started working out with him, I could do one. If I jumped first. Now I could do three and was struggling to make four my new PR.

I groaned as my muscles strained to lift my body one more time. Sweat trickled down the back of my neck and my stomach clenched, trying to give my exhausted arms a boost. My arms straightened, and I was about to let go when Ledger stood in front of me and grabbed onto the bar.

"Wrap your legs around my waist," he said.

"What? Why?" I asked.

He smiled. "Do you trust me?"

"Yes." I drew out the word as I watched him. His shirt was off and normally I would be grossed out by someone else's sweaty body touching me, but I wasn't minding it too much right now.

"I think I need to add some Aladdin role playing to my bucket list now," he said.

I snorted and rolled my eyes. This guy and his Disney obsession. I wrapped my legs around his waist as he requested. I wasn't sure if I wanted to cheer at this new position and run away from how much I liked it. Our bodies were pressed together before, but now it was even more so.

"Now pull." Ledger's voice was husky as he stared into my eyes.

I tightened my legs and pulled him closer to me.

"Nope, not that way," Ledger said. His eyes squeezed shut, and he took a deep breath.

Oh, he meant up. I looked up at the bar so I wouldn't have to meet his eyes when he opened them again. Why did I assume he meant pull in any other way? Hopefully, he would assume my red cheeks were still from my workout.

When I tried pulling up this time, Ledger pulled himself up with me. With my legs wrapped around him, he helped me lift myself up. I was able to pump out seven more to make it to ten pull-ups for the day. I was pretty sure he did about eighty percent of the work on the last three or four, but I chose to ignore that.

After I unwrapped my legs from around Ledger, we both dropped from the bar. I squealed and launched myself at him.

"New PR," I said, while squeezing his neck.

"If you have this much strength left in your arms, maybe we should do a few more," he teased. He returned my hug even tighter, making me laugh and wiggle in his arms. I slid down the front of him when he finally relaxed his hold on me. Our eyes met and the playfulness was gone.

Once again, I was aware of his state of undress and mine. Leggings and a tank top tended not to hide much.

"You did great, doll." Ledger's hand rested on my hips. The tips of his fingers grazed the top of my ass.

"I think you did most of it during the end," I said, my voice barely above a whisper.

"And I didn't mind it one bit."

I knew he wasn't referring to the pullups.

"Neither did I," I admitted. My hands rested on his biceps and I fought the urge to run them down his chest and abs.

"Are you guys done in here?"

I jumped back; the spell broken with Dorian's annoyance.

"I'm going to go shower," I said to no one in particular and hightailed it out of there.

"Damn cock blocker," Ledger said as I raced up the stairs.

"Put a shell on the door next time or something," Dorian replied.

* * *

Jem always seemed to anticipate my needs before I voiced them. The week I started my period, he gave me a gift basket filled with bath bombs, candles, and chocolates. He always voted in my favor for which movies to watch. A couple of days after I showed up, a hand-crafted mug with a turtle etched on it showed up and sat on the counter, ready for my hot chocolate or tea every morning. There was even a separate hazelnut creamer with my name written on it in the fridge. Although that might have been more for Dorian's sake than mine, I was okay to share.

One of my favorite times was late at night when Jem was composing new songs for their next album on the piano in his room and I got to relax on his bed doing my work. The other guys were usually gone for a midnight swim, something they did often, but never all together. Someone was always home with me. Never Dorian, though. I think they were worried one of us would be gone if he was left home with me.

While I was scheduling posts for a local baker on Instagram, Jem sighed and threw his pencil at the wall.

"Hey, you doing okay?" I asked. I closed my laptop and got off the bed, walking over to rub Jem's shoulders.

"Yeah, I just can't get the chorus right. There's something missing, but I'm not sure what." He leaned back against me and groaned. "Your hands feel great."

I chuckled and gave his neck a few more quick squeezes. "Play it for me."

"Play what?" His eyes were closed, and his head was resting against my chest.

"The chorus. Sometimes an outside ear helps." I sat on the edge of his piano bench.

"What do you know about music?" he asked. His eyes went wide. "Shit, I didn't mean it like that, Lyss."

"You're fine," I laughed. "I dabbled some in high school and college."

"Oh, yeah? What did you play?" He scooted over to make more room for me.

"I did choir and violin."

"You any good?"

I shrugged and picked up the sheet music he had been writing on. "Not bad. Enough for it to get me a scholarship until I officially changed my major to marketing."

"Can you sight read?"

"I can give it a shot." I picked out the melody on the piano to get the tune, then read through the lyrics, humming lightly. After feeling like I had the general melody down, I nodded to Jem that I was ready, and he started playing the piano. I sang along with it quietly at first. It had been a couple years since I had sight read anything and I didn't want to sound like a complete moron in front of the cute guy who did this for a living.

His nod of encouragement when I looked to him for reassurance gave me more confidence and my voice was stronger going into the next chorus.

I made a couple of suggestions about the lyrics. Jem grabbed a new pencil, erased some parts and rewrote them, nodding the whole time.

We ran through it several more times. Jem pointed out things that sounded off and I would make a suggestion. I would mention something that could use something different and he would play a few different bars until we decided on what would be best.

By the end, Jem was grinning from ear to ear.

"That's it, that's what it was missing," he said.

I grinned. "Glad I could help."

"Why did you stop?"

I sighed deeply and played with the hem of my shirt. "I had other dreams that I didn't want to chance not being fulfilled if I stayed with music. Besides, it's a fun hobby, but it was never something I was super serious about."

"What other dreams do you have? I can't imagine being a social media manager to a group of guys was one of them."

"Far from it," I agreed with a laugh. "No, I want to travel and see the world on my schedule. Someday, I want to meet a guy and fall in love and travel the world with him and a suitcase. Marketing is such a broad major that there are a ton of directions I could go with it. I could work from home, I could join a large corporation, the possibilities are endless. I ended up doing social media management because it's something I'm good at and it gives me the flexibility to work a normal job for a steady income until I build up my clientele."

"Sounds like your plan is coming along nicely."

"You guys were a surprise, but one I'm pretty happy with so far."

"I just hope you don't find your dream guy anytime soon."

"Why's that?" I played a few chords on the piano, pleased I was able to be a part in creating a beautiful new song.

"Because I would have to get rid of him."

I looked over and was startled to see Jem's face so close to mine, yet I didn't move away.

"Get rid of him?" I asked.

He nodded. "I don't know if I could give you up right now, my little siren."

"I don't think I want you to." My voice was a whisper, and I leaned closer to Jem.

He had been keeping his distance. They all had really, even Ledger with as much as he flirted. He never said anything to make me uncomfortable and whenever he touched me, it was nothing that would get him in trouble at a high school dance. Aside from our moment in the gym. And that kiss he gave me when I agreed to work with them. Thinking of the kiss made me lick my lips, and I saw Jem's eyes dart down.

He lifted a hand to brush my hair away from my face, and I shivered when he trailed his fingers down and around the back of my neck.

"Lyss?"

"Yeah?" I whispered. My eyes were half closed as they stared into his.

"Can I kiss you?"

"Please."

His hand tightened on my neck and pulled me forward. The second his lips touched mine, I was a goner. I sighed into his mouth and brought my hands up to his chest. His head tilted to the side to deepen our kiss. My tongue darted out to taste his lips, and he groaned. His hands grasped my hips and pulled me on top of him to straddle him. I buried a hand in his hair to keep him close. Our tongues danced together and his hands went under my shirt to rub my back and stroke my waist.

I ground my hips against him, my thin pajama shorts and his sweat pants doing very little to hide his growing excitement. His hands reached up to brush the underside of my breast and I gasped. My head fell back, and he kissed his way down my neck. I pulled at his shirt, desperate to feel his skin against me. We broke apart just long enough for me to pull it over his head and toss it to the side. His muscles bunched under my touch as I rubbed my hands all over his torso, feeling every peak and valley of his sculpted body. His hands reached around my back to unhook my bra, but I was wearing a bralette. Just as he was about to push it up and free my aching breasts, a door slammed shut.

"Honeys, we're home," Ledger sang.

Jem and I froze and stared at each other, panting.

"We shouldn't be doing this," I whispered, leaning my forehead against his.

"I'm sorry if I pushed you too hard."

I shook my head and leaned back just enough so I could stare into his eyes. "We shouldn't do this," I repeated. "But I don't regret it. You didn't push me into anything at all. If you remember, I was the one who started pulling clothes off of you."

He chuckled and squeezed my thighs gently. If I thought my nipples were hard and ready for some action, they had nothing on the damp part of me that was pressed intimately against something of Jem's.

"I like you, Lyss."

"And I like you, but I can't do this while I'm working for you. And how weird would it be for the other guys knowing we were together?"

"Not as weird as you think."

I looked at him questioningly. What did he mean? Did he call dibs on me? Did the others already think we were together? I was getting ahead of myself. They had been nothing but gentlemen since I got here. Well, excluding Dorian. He was still an asshole.

"I'm just going to go to my room." I slid slowly off his lap and grabbed my laptop. He waited a minute before standing up and walking me to my room.

"Hey, thanks for your help on the song," he said when we were in front of my bedroom door.

I smiled, feeling shy all of a sudden. "It was fun. Let me know if you want help again."

Jem looked down the hall before leaning down and stealing a kiss. "Goodnight, Lyss."

I watched him walk back to his room just across from mine and closed the door before I went into my room.

"Oh, Lyss. How are you going to handle this one?" I asked myself.

Chapter 10

Rook

I was adding flour to a bowl to make biscuits when Lyss came out of her room to join me. It was our own little routine each morning to make breakfast together, and I loved it. She was usually wearing those little matchy pajamas that she favored. No t-shirt and gym shorts for her, just shorts that showed off her long, toned legs and a matching top that showed her nipples every time she was a little cold. Or aroused. After the first couple of weeks, she even stopped worrying about trying to fix her hair before coming out of her room. She either had it thrown up in that messy bun girls did so effortlessly or left it down like she did today, looking like she had been thoroughly fucked the night before.

Jem had told us about their make-out session last night and her worry about the rest of us finding out. We had all talked about it before. Well, not Dorian. He was still trying to push Lyss away, but he had his reasons. The other three of us, though, all agreed that we liked Lyss and wouldn't be upset if she decided she liked one of us. But if she ended up liking all of us, well, that would be a bonus for us and for her.

She was humming quietly as she looked for the ground pork in the fridge and her hips were shaking to the beat. I gripped the pastry cutter a little tighter as I mixed the butter into the flour mixture. I couldn't count how many times I had imagined grabbing those lush hips of hers and putting her on the counter so I could sink into her.

I stayed close to the edge of the counter as she walked past me. No sense in showing her how I was feeling right now.

"Morning." Lyss patted me on the arm as she walked by.

From the time she met me, she hadn't been afraid. Most people were. Where we were from, they knew why they should be. Here they didn't know, but they kept their distance, like fish when they scented a shark in the water. Not Lyss, though. Even when she had to convince me to stop beating on some worthless guy that had attacked her.

"Jem said he had a nice surprise from you last night," I said nonchalantly.

Lyss pulled the pan out and sat it on the stove. I knew her cheeks were turning pink already.

"I, um, yeah. It shouldn't have happened. It wasn't Jem's fault, it was mine." She stumbled over her words. Even though I couldn't see her face, I knew she was chewing on her thumbnail right now.

"I was talking about the music. Did something else happen?" I pretended ignorance and tried not to laugh.

I could feel her worry and when I looked over my shoulder at her, she was opening and closing her mouth as she struggled with an excuse. I put a finger under her chin and pushed softly to close her mouth. Her brows were pinched over her wide eyes as she looked at me.

"Don't think I've ever seen you so flustered, little guppy. Jem also mentioned you guys kissed. You know we don't keep secrets around here."

She tried to look away, but I didn't move my finger from her chin, forcing her to keep facing me.

"I just don't want to ruin the dynamic between you guys," she whispered.

I smiled. She was so worried about ruining things she couldn't see how head over heels we all were for her.

"You won't ruin anything. We've all been together long enough that there isn't much that would get between us. I know Jem likes you. If you like him, I don't see anything wrong with it. You're both adults." It pained me a little to give her to Jem so easily, but if we wanted anything to work out with one or all of us, she needed to know that we really were okay with it.

Lyss studied my face before asking, "What if I like more than just him, though?"

I fought to keep my face neutral. I knew she liked all of us, but to hear it from her lips, even in a roundabout way, was glorious.

"If that's the case, then you'll find that more than just Jem like you. Like I said, we've been together for a long time. You don't get as close as we are without learning to share." I went back to my biscuits, leaving her with that little remark to chew on for a bit.

I finished the biscuit dough, spread some flour on the counter and prepped it to cut into circles.

Ledger came into the kitchen yawning. He walked right up to Lyss and wrapped his arms around her waist. Out of all of us, he was the one who had got to touch her the most, and I wasn't afraid to admit I was a little jealous, but that was just his personality. It didn't bother Lyss, so I didn't worry about it much.

"Mornin' doll." His voice was still rough with sleep and he nuzzled his face into Lyss's neck.

Nothing new there, but what was new was the soft moan Lyss let out. We all froze. My cock was at full attention now.

"Gravy's done," Lyss announced, her voice higher than normal. She turned and handed Ledger the spoon she had been using. "Stir it for a couple more minutes so it doesn't burn. Rook can help if you need it."

"Where are you going, little guppy?" I asked with a smirk.

"I, um, I need to—I've gotta wash my hair." She pointed to her head. Her cheeks were bright pink now. She was walking backwards as she talked to me and ran into Jem.

"Hey, Lyss." He smiled, and I knew he was replaying his kiss with her from last night through his head. Lucky bastard.

She squeaked out a hi and practically ran to her room.

"What just happened?" Jem asked. His hair was sticking up from all different angles. That was part of the reason I kept mine so short. No need to worry about styling it.

"She moaned," Ledger said, still staring in the direction Lyss had run.

"She what?" Jem looked back and forth between me and Ledger.

"I gave her a hug and she moaned." A smile was forming on Ledger's face now.

"Are you sure you didn't squeeze her too hard or something?"

"Nope. I hugged her and rubbed my nose on her neck and she moaned."

"Gravy," I reminded him. He was looking too damn proud of himself.

He started stirring the gravy while Jem settled in on a stool.

"She may have mentioned that she likes more than just Jem." I used the biscuit cutter to cut the dough into perfect circles.

"May have?" Ledger asked, forgetting about the gravy again.

I shrugged. "And I may have told her that Jem wasn't the only one interested in her. I may have also mentioned that she didn't have to just choose one if she didn't want to." I put the biscuits on a sheet pan and moved them to the oven that had been preheating.

"Rook, I love you, man, but I'm about to beat the shit out of you if you don't quit messing around." Ledger stared me down.

I smiled. He might be our trainer, but we both knew I would win. He had the fancy moves, but he taught me those and then, adding in my brute strength, I would wipe the floor with him.

"I told her we knew how to share when we needed to and she didn't seem offended by the idea." I crossed my arms and leaned against the counter.

Ledger nodded his head. "If we go off of that moan that still has me hard, I'd say she might even be pro-sharing."

Now they were getting it. I grinned. "I think the little guppy might be caught in our net."

"And we're not letting her out of it," Jem said.

No, we were not. This one woman had us all wrapped around her little finger and didn't even know it yet, but she would soon enough.

Chapter 11

Lyss

I hid out in my room the rest of the day. It was technically one of my days off, so I didn't need to be doing anything. I skipped breakfast to have a cold shower, which did absolutely nothing to help with mixed feelings. I wanted to ask the guys my questions, but how would I even bring that up? What if I totally misunderstood what Rook meant? What if it made things super awkward between us all? On top of all that, I was working for them. There were rules about not dating co-workers for a reason. I was pretty sure that went double when you were living with them.

There were too many things that could go wrong and nothing guaranteed to go right. I just needed to get over it. Yeah, I knew Jem was interested. That was kind of obvious with what happened last night. Who knew how long that would last, though? It might have just been a moment that we both got caught up in. At least for him. I knew I liked him, but he had hundreds, if not thousands, of adoring fans wishing he would tear their panties off with his teeth. Okay, there was only one that had voiced that, but I knew there were others that were thinking it. Hell, I know I was.

Ledger knocked on my door to ask if I wanted to watch a movie. I declined, claiming a headache. It was a cliche for a reason; it worked. Jem stopped by later and left lunch by my door. I waited until I heard him go into his room and close the door before I opened mine to bring the tray in. It was a sandwich with a bag of chips, grapes, and a can of my favorite soda. He even included a piece of chocolate from the bag I kept hidden in the pantry. Guess I didn't hide it as well as I thought.

I watched Netflix on my laptop, got some work done, read a book, and just relaxed. It was quite nice, even if I knew I was just being a wimp. I ignored that part, though. Thank heavens it was Rook's turn for dinner tonight. I wasn't sure I could face the guys right now. I was giving myself one day to get my hormones together.

After night fell, Jem knocked on my door again.

"You feeling any better, Lyss?"

Guilt churned in my stomach at the concern in his voice. Why couldn't I just be one of those brave, ballsy girls like in the books I read, who just told the guys she was interested in that she was into them and seduced them with her sex appeal? Oh, right. Because I was most comfortable behind a screen.

"Yeah, I think I'm just going to go to bed early tonight." I yawned loudly to emphasize how tired I was. Not.

"Okay. Rook, Ledger, and I are going out for a swim. Dorian will be here if you need him. We figured that with you guys both locking yourselves in your rooms, you guys should be fine alone for a few hours. Rook made spaghetti for dinner. There's a plate in the microwave for you if you want it."

"Thanks, Jem. You guys be safe out there tonight." It was the same thing I told them every night. Why they waited until dark to go swimming in the ocean was beyond me. Maybe because there was less worry about being recognized while out there. They had private access to the water, so it was usually pretty secluded, but sometimes people went by in their boats. Still, who knew what creatures came out at night in the water? I was perfectly content to just use the pool.

It was quiet for a moment and I assumed he had left. I opened my Kindle app to continue reading when he spoke again.

"Hey, Lyss?"

"Yeah?"

"Can I come in for a second?"

All of them had stuck to the rule that my room was my room. This was the first time any of them had asked to come in. I scanned the room to make sure it wasn't too big of a mess. Some clothes were on the floor and I threw them in the closet, closing the door to hide them.

"You can come in now," I said.

The door opened slowly, and Jem stepped in, closing it behind him. He was already in his swim trunks, his chest bare, and I swallowed to bring some moisture back to my mouth.

"I just wanted to make sure you were really okay." He rubbed the back of his neck.

I nodded my head. "Yeah, I just needed a mental break today."

"Does it have anything to do with last night?"

I shook my head in denial, then realized it would be stupid to lie. If we all expected to live together, we couldn't keep secrets, just like Rook said. That included me.

"A little," I admitted.

Jem's eyebrows pinched together in concern.

"I don't regret it at all or feel uncomfortable around you," I quickly reassured him. "I like you, Jem, I really do."

He breathed a sigh of relief and stepped closer to me. My head tilted back to look up at him. All the guys were so tall and I wasn't short, at just over five and a half feet.

"Then what's the problem, siren?"

"Sirens lure men to their death with their voice. I hardly qualify as that." I took a small step towards him.

"Maybe not to the death, but your voice is a siren call all the same. I'd follow wherever it led me."

I chuckled. "That sounds like something Ledger would say."

He winced and smiled. "It was pretty cheesy, wasn't it? Still true though. So, are you going to tell me what the problem is with both of us enjoying last night?" His fingers reached out to brush against mine.

I could feel the blush creeping in. Was I just going to be a permanent shade of pink or red around these guys?

"I like you," I began slowly. "But I don't like *just* you."

"Is this what's been bothering you this whole time?" he asked.

I nodded my head. "Mainly. I also worry about ruining the friendships I've created with you guys. Well, with three of you."

"You think I haven't noticed how your eyes light up when Ledger spins you around the room? Or how comfortable you are with Rook when most people stay ten feet away from him for fear he'll crush their skulls? Or even the sexual tension when you and Dorian are verbally sparring?"

"There is no sexual tension between Dorian and I. He's an asshole." I crossed my arms and noticed his eyes dip down to my pushed up breasts briefly.

"He's only an asshole to you. He's always been the type to pull on the pigtails of the girls he likes."

"Whatever. I've seen how he is with other girls. Some extremely attractive ones. You going to tell me he has liked none of them?"

"For sex, sure. It's the ones he likes beyond the physical that he doesn't know how to act around."

I scoffed. "If you say so."

Jem chuckled. "Back to our original topic. Don't feel bad about liking the other guys. We don't feel bad about all liking you."

All? Did he just say they all liked me? Like, *liked me,* liked me? I figured Ledger was just a flirt with anyone with boobs, and Rook tolerated me. After our talk this morning, though, didn't he admit he liked me in a roundabout way?

"That's part of the problem, though." I turned my back towards Jem in frustration. "I like you guys, you guys like me, but how do I pick one? What if I do, but I can't get over the other two? What if it causes animosity between you guys? I came here to be your social media manager, not worm my way into your bed or break up the band."

"You're overthinking this. You don't."

"I don't what?"

"You don't pick."

I looked over my shoulder at him. "I'm going to need you to be very clear on that, so I don't misunderstand you."

Jem laughed and ran his fingers through his hair. "You don't pick one of us. We all like you, and if you like all of us, why should you pick?"

"Because that's just how things are," I sputtered.

"You mean because monogamy is a societal norm?"

I nodded.

"So is smoking, drinking, and eating rocky mountain oysters."

I scrunched my nose up at the last one, causing him to laugh again.

"I've never seen you smoke. You don't drink, and bull testicles don't seem to appeal to you. Are you weird for not liking those? Do you look down on those that do?"

"Of course not. It's just a preference."

"Exactly." Jem smiled. "So why should you care what society says about your relationship preference?"

Everything he said made sense. Could it really be this easy?

"I don't like to share," I said. "I wouldn't be able to handle one of you going out with someone else if we were together."

"Then we wouldn't," he said simply. "I have no interest in juggling multiple partners. That's why I'm not trying to push this on you. I just want you to consider it. It's not for everybody and there's no shame in that."

"Wouldn't you guys get jealous, though? What if I spend too much time with one of you and not the other? Would the others even agree to it?"

"I wouldn't be talking about it with you if I hadn't already talked to them about it. You have all of us under your spell." He leaned against the door with his arms crossed.

I gnawed on my thumbnail.

"And sure, we might get jealous occasionally, but we'll communicate. Some women get jealous of their partner's video game console. But they talk about it and work it out."

"This is a lot," I admitted. "It just seems too good to be true. For me anyway. What do you guys get out of this? I get three sexy as hell guys, but you all have to share one girl?"

Jem pushed off the door and walked to me to put his hands on my shoulder. "We get you, siren. That's plenty and all we want. Can I kiss you before I leave?"

"You don't have to ask my permission every time," I said, tilting my head up and putting my arms around his waist.

"Until I'm sure you are completely comfortable with this, I do. You hold all the control here, Lyss." He stared into my eyes so seriously that my heart couldn't help but melt a little.

"In that case, yes, you can kiss me." I stood up on my tiptoes to meet him halfway.

Unlike our explosive kiss yesterday, this one was sweet.

"I better go before I get much more into this," he said.

I giggled and leaned up for one more quick peck.

"Think about what we talked about," he said as he opened the door.

I nodded. "I will."

With one last smile, he left, closing the door behind him.

Chapter 12

Lyss

After Jem and the others left, I took a bath. Something about water was always so calming. I filled the tub and threw in a bath bomb. I brought my Kindle in with me and downloaded a reverse harem book to read. Best way to learn is to read after all.

I stayed in for about an hour, just relaxing and reading. The book addressed some of the same concerns I had with a potential polyamorous relationship, but they seemed to overcome each obstacle exactly how Jem had said, communication. One of the guys in the group wasn't too thrilled with the idea of sharing, but he eventually came around to the idea if that was what he needed to do to keep the girl. This group of guys didn't even know each other at first, and they all somehow made it work. My guys were all good friends already.

Water sloshed over the edge of the tub. My guys. I had just called them my guys. When did they go from *the* guys to *my* guys? I pulled the plug to let the water out and got out of the tub. I dried off and wrapped the towel around me. My hair was in a topknot, and I pulled my scrunchie out, letting it fall over my shoulders. Normally it was stick straight, but it had some waves from being bunched up on the top of my head after my shower this morning.

I changed into my pajamas and turned off the light before crawling into bed. I really should make it an early night. As I laid there, though, sleep wouldn't come. Thoughts of dating one of the guys I'd been living with raced through my head and thoughts of dating all of them overwhelmed me.

A loud rumble of thunder had me turning towards the door to my balcony. I pushed my covers off and got out of bed. It was too quiet in here. I opened the door to the balcony so the sounds of the light rainfall and the smell of ocean air filled my room. The moon was full tonight, peeking through the clouds every so often.

There was a slight breeze, but I didn't pull my blankets back on. I closed my eyes and the memory of Jem's lips made mine tingle. My right hand slid up my stomach, pulling my tank top with it. The memory of Jem's hands on me last night, rubbing right under my breasts, filled my head. My imagination continued with what he would have done if the guys returning hadn't interrupted us. I pulled my top up over my breasts and brushed a finger over my nipple softly. I sighed, then moaned when I pinched it and rolled it between my fingers.

My legs scissored together as I continued playing with my nipples. I could feel myself growing wet. With Jem already active in my imagination, Ledger joined him, nuzzling into that sweet spot on my neck like he did this morning. I kicked my shorts and panties off and spread my legs. My right hand kept playing with my nipples, alternating between the two, and my left hand reached between my legs. I groaned as I dipped two fingers into my pussy and rubbed the juices over my clit.

My fingers moved in slow circles as I pictured being sandwiched between Jem and Ledger, our naked skin sliding against each other. I pinched my nipple again and pulled slightly, imagining Jem sucking on it. In my head, Ledger pinched my clit and my hips bucked towards his hand.

I was breathing heavily, but I knew my hands wouldn't give me the explosive orgasm I was seeking. I blindly reached for the nightstand and pulled out the small bag that held my womanizer. If I opened my eyes, I was worried the fantasy I had been building up in my head would disappear.

The womanizer was quiet when I first turned it on. After turning it up a couple of notches, I placed it against my swollen clit. My head pushed back into the pillows. I kept it at that speed for a minute before turning it up again.

Rook joined my fantasy and was going down on me. His tongue swirling and sucking my clit while Jem and Ledger alternated between kissing me and sucking my nipples. I was close to coming, but wasn't ready for it to end yet, so I pulled the vibrator away until I could calm down for a minute. I returned it to its position and let it build up again. Just as I was getting close to coming, something made me open my eyes.

Dorian was standing in my doorway, basketball shorts, no shirt, both hands braced on either side of the doorjamb, staring at me with intense hunger in his eyes. I sat up with a gasp, closing my legs and covering my bare breasts while I panted heavily. I was so close! If I squeezed my legs together, I would probably come.

"Don't stop," Dorian demanded, his voice low and gravelly. His hair was flat against his head as the rain continued to come down outside. "Lean against the headboard and spread those legs."

If I wasn't so desperate to come, I wouldn't have listened to him. Or so I told myself. I scooted back, so the headboard propped me up and spread my legs as he commanded.

"Turn towards me a little more so I can watch that wet pussy spasm when you come."

I didn't think I was one for dirty talk, but holy shit, he was getting me hot. I adjusted my body, so he had a clear view of my pussy.

"Turn the setting down low and put it back on you."

I didn't need to ask what 'it' was. I turned down the intensity and put the vibrator back on my clit. I closed my eyes and leaned my head back.

"Open your eyes and look at me," he said.

I opened my eyes and glared at him.

He chuckled. "Good girl," he growled.

I almost came from that alone, but it was still too low. I was about to turn it up, but Dorian stopped me.

"No. I want to watch you squirm for a bit."

I was already so close, but I couldn't quite come. I groaned in frustration and wiggled my hips against the bed. My free hand came back to my nipples, hoping the extra stimulation would push me over the edge.

Dorian groaned, low and long. "Damn, flower. You're killing me over here with that cunt wide open for me. Do you want some help and a bigger finish?"

My muscles were tense to the point of almost cramping because I wanted to come so badly. Dorian was palming his extremely erect cock through his shorts. I could only imagine what he could do to me with that thing. Did I want my first time with one of the guys to be with him, though? The asshole that had done nothing to deserve me, so I shook my head.

He frowned, but remained where he was standing. "When you come, I want you to say my name. Can you do that, flower?"

I nodded desperately. I would do almost anything to come at this point. Lightning shot across the sky, illuminating his outline, but plunging his beautiful face into the shadows. Thunder followed the lightning, and I could almost feel it in my chest.

"Turn that thing up five times."

I pressed the increase button five times and my orgasm ripped through me. I screamed at the intensity of it.

"My name," Dorian demanded.

I debated if I should give him the satisfaction of listening to him. His bossy commands had helped me reach this point though, and I was curious to see what effect I had on him. I gasped his name as a smaller orgasm reached its peak.

"Keep your eyes on me," Dorian said. The man was so demanding and damn if I didn't find it hot as hell right now.

I hadn't even realized my eyes had closed. I forced them open and locked eyes with him. His eyes were hungry, and I could tell he was fighting to stay outside of my room.

"Beautiful," he murmured. "Say my name again."

Another orgasm shot through me and I arched my back, reaching behind me to hold on to the headboard.

"Dorian," I cried out.

"Keep it on there."

"I can't." I panted through gritted teeth. I was already so sensitive that it was bordering on pain.

"Yes, you can," he reassured me.

I held the vibrator where it was, my legs shaking, sweat coating my body until a fourth orgasm made me scream again. I pushed the toy away from me and collapsed against the bed. Never had I had such an intense orgasm, or set of orgasms, and the damn man didn't even have to touch me once.

Chapter 13

Dorian

My cock was painfully hard as I watched Lyss lay panting on the bed. I'd only come out onto the deck for some fresh air and to watch the storm. I hadn't even planned on going near her room. Not until I heard her gasp and whimper. I was the only one here with her, what if she was hurt? I peeked into her room only to see that it was a toy making her make those sounds.

I debated walking away, but I couldn't. It was her fault for doing it with the door open. I wasn't in her room. I wasn't breaking any of her rules. When she realized I was there, I had expected her to scream at me and slam the door in my face.

But she didn't. She made me stay outside in the pouring rain, which I knew I deserved, but she listened to me. She came for me. She screamed my name. And it was one of the most beautiful things I had ever seen or heard. It was a test of my willpower, to stay out of her room as I watched those orgasms rip through her. My cock had never been so hard.

When her breathing had slowed, she sat up and pulled her shirt down before slipping back into her shorts, forgoing her panties. I almost moaned as she walked towards me, knowing that those little shorts were the only things covering her bare pussy.

"Enjoy the show?" She crossed her arms and tried to appear nonchalant.

I grinned down at her hungrily. "Immensely."

"Good, you can leave now. I'm ready for bed and you're blocking the breeze." She pushed at my chest and I grabbed her hand as I took a quick step back. She stumbled and fell right into my arms.

"The real question is, did you enjoy yourself?" I traced a lazy figure eight on the back of her hand.

"It got the job done, scratched an itch." She shrugged a shoulder, but I felt her shiver when my hand traced up her arm to caress her inner elbow. She didn't even flinch at standing in the rain. The water soaking through her clothes, exposing her still-hard nipples.

I laughed. "Don't lie to me, flower. I bet if my hand went underneath those tiny shorts of yours, I would find you dripping. Your cheeks are still flushed, your breathing is still ragged, and I bet your legs are weak from shaking so much."

She just glared at me and I knew it was because everything I had said was spot on.

Because I was still a little bitter she hadn't let me come in to help her finish, I leaned down and whispered into her ear. "Just remember the first orgasms you had with one of us were with me and it was my name you screamed."

She tried pulling away, but I wrapped my other arm around her back, keeping her flush against me. There was no doubt she could feel my erection with how close we were and damn if I didn't love her wiggling against it. I leaned back far enough to look at her pissed-off face.

"And I didn't even have to touch you."

She snarled and broke free. "You are such an asshole!"

"So you keep telling me, but this asshole's name sounded hella good coming from your lips."

"Don't act like I was the only one enjoying it," she seethed.

"What? No one around to warm your bed so you have to watch the one person you can't stand to get your rocks off?" She laughed, but it was bitter. "Glad to have something new for your spank bank, Dory?"

If only what she was saying was true. If I really couldn't stand her, this whole situation would be a lot easier. I should have said no as my final word when the others voted for her to stay, but apparently, I liked to torture myself. Just like I did tonight, watching her even knowing I couldn't touch her.

She turned to go back into her room, but I pulled on her hand again since I hadn't let it go, and she fell back into my arms. We were both completely soaked. I wished the water would have made Lyss less attractive, but all it did was accentuate her beauty. Droplets clung to her eyelashes, making her eyes sparkle even more. The water plastered her hair against her head, but that just let me focus on the gentle curves and angles of her face. I especially loved how her clothes clung to her body.

"You're not in your safety bubble anymore, flower. And your guard dogs are gone. It's just you and me."

Lyss pushed against my chest again. I simply gathered both her hands into one of mine and lifted them up before I pulled them down behind her head. I applied just a little more pressure, so she was arching against me. She still fought to get free, only stopping when I leaned my head back and moaned at her rubbing up against me.

"You told me once that you might like it a little rough. Have you decided if you have?" I slid my free hand along the side of her hip. "You sure listen to directions awful well."

Lightning lit up the sky and I could see her pupils were wide. She dropped her gaze to my lips before her little pink tongue reached out to swipe across her lower lip. She was as turned on as I was. Lyss shook her head, but her body rubbed against mine. I leaned forward, invading her space.

"Tell me to stop, Lyss," I pleaded in a whisper, my lips millimeters away from hers.

My hand moved to her hip, up to her waist, stopping just under her breast. Her breath hitched, and she stared at me as if daring me to continue my journey upwards.

"What are we doing?" Her voice shook slightly. "We can't stand each other."

I was quiet for a minute. I should let her continue to believe that, let myself continue to pretend to believe that. But after what I just watched her do and having her body pressed against mine, I couldn't lie to either of us anymore.

"It's not you I can't stand. I can't have you and I hate it, so it's me I can't stand." I let go of her hands. She brought them forward slowly to rest on my shoulders.

"Why can't you have me?"

I chuckled. "Greedy little flower, aren't you? I know the others already talked to you about pursuing a relationship."

Lyss ducked her head and took a step back, but I pulled her back to me.

"I've tried to keep my distance. I've tried to push you away so you wouldn't tempt me, but I'm only so strong."

Her eyes were wide and beautiful as she stared up at me.

"Give me one night," I said, surprising the both of us.

"Dorian—"

"All I can give you is one night. If you're willing to give it to me."

I watched her lower lip get sucked in between her teeth as she thought. I ran my hand over her hair, tucking it behind her ear. Would she accept my offer? Would she even want to after the way I treated her? I hadn't been fair to her, just so I could prevent myself from hurting. I never should have asked her. It was selfish of me.

Lyss finally opened her mouth, but I never got to hear if she was going to agree or turn me down because Jem yelled from the dining room.

Chapter 14

Lyss

"Dorian! We need you!"

The urgency in Jem's voice was like a bucket of ice cold water being dumped on me. Dorian swore under his breath as he let me go and we both rushed into my room to go through the door that led to the living room.

Ledger was lying on the table and there was blood everywhere. They were all still soaking wet. And completely naked. What the hell did those boys do when they went swimming?

"What happened?" Dorian asked.

"Crataeisians showed up while we were out. They grazed him with a spear," Rook spat out. "And they had sharks with them."

I gasped. The shredded wound on Ledger's arm was... a shark bite? Just below his ribs on the same side as his injured arm was a large gash from what I now knew was a spear.

Dorian swore again and went to the sink to wash his hands.

"Dorian, they said 'Ceto is rising.'" Jem said.

"They always say that." Dorian rolled his eyes and dried off his hands.

"No, they say usually say 'Ceto *will* rise,'" Jem corrected. "This time she said she *is* rising."

"Who's Ceto?" I asked.

Jem, Rook, and Dorian all turned to look at me as if they had forgotten I was there.

"Brief me after. Jem, get the first aid kit. Rook, towels and water. Then get some pants on for Triton's sake."

Rook and Jem hurried to do what Dorian commanded.

"Shouldn't we call the police? An ambulance? Take him to the hospital?" I asked.

"No." Dorian gently probed Ledger's side and arm, checking every puncture.

I washed my hands at the sink and came to stand by the table.

"What can I do then?" I asked.

"Nothing, just go back to your room, Amaryllis." Dorian didn't even bother looking at me as he examined Ledger.

So we were back to this already. I leaned a hip on the side of the table, next to Ledger's uninjured arm.

"No."

Dorian looked up at me, his eyes narrowing. "Are you disobeying me?"

"First off, I have no reason to obey you. Second, my friend is hurt and I want to help. So you're going to let me help."

"Let her help, Dorian," Rook said, coming back with towels.

Dorian glared at me and I glared right back. "Fine. You can clean his arm unless the blood is too much for you."

I moved to the other side of the table where Dorian was standing. "Sweetie, I bleed for a week every month. I can handle a little blood."

Rook snorted a laugh and Jem came back with the first-aid kit. The box was closer to the size of a suitcase than the little red plastic box I was expecting. An IV pole and several IV bags of liquid were in his other hand. He set up the pole and the bags next to Ledger's uninjured arm before searching through the large first aid kit for IV tubing. He hooked everything up together before getting a needle to insert it into Ledger's arm and using medical tape to secure it. After making sure the bags were flowing correctly, he got a syringe, used it to measure something out of a glass vial, and shot it into one of the ports.

A bowl of water appeared between me and Dorian. I picked up a clean washcloth and started dabbing the blood from Ledger's arm.

"I'm going to do a perimeter search," Rook announced.

"Not alone. Take Jem with you. Amaryllis is here if I need help."

Both men, now clad in shorts and t-shirts, nodded and went back out the door.

Dorian and I worked in silence. I finished cleaning Ledger's arm and was wrapping it tightly with gauze until Dorian could get to it and make sure it didn't need stitches.

"Hey, doll, what are you doing under the water? You'll drown, you know? You need to be an oceanid to survive down here."

When did Ledger wake up? I looked at Dorian, unsure of what to do.

"He's hallucinating from the pain meds Jem gave him," Dorian said.

Ledger looked down. "Dory! You're here too! I never thought I'd see the five of us under the sea together." He looked to his left as Dorian groaned at the nickname. "Look, that singing crab from the cartoon is here! Under the sea! Doo-do-do-doo. Under the sea!"

"Is he singing with Sebastian from The Little Mermaid?" I asked.

Dorian sighed and nodded. "For some reason, he thinks the movie is hilarious even though it is the furthest thing from reality."

"Well, duh, it's a cartoon, and it's about a mermaid. What part of that screams reality to you?" I laughed.

Dorian cleared his throat and didn't answer. He tied the last stich in the wound on Ledger's side and started unwrapping his arm.

"You sure we shouldn't take him to the hospital? Shark bites can be lethal just due to the amount of bacteria from their teeth."

A humorless laugh escaped Dorian. "Trust me, flower, I know all about shark bites, and a hospital isn't going to help him one bit."

I clenched my jaw to keep from replying. Ledger needed our help right now, not us bickering.

Ledger lifted his arm up to look at it. "Whoa, I've got a bunch of little holes in me. It's like I've been shot a hundred times."

"You were bit, dumbass, now lay back down." Dorian's words lacked any bite as he pushed down on his friend's chest.

"Bit?" He looked at me with a big grin. "Doll, did you bite me because I look good enough to eat?"

I couldn't help but laugh. "Yup, my mouth is that big with that many pointy teeth."

Ledger's eyes got huge, and he looked horrified. "You're never sucking my dick, then. I can't lose that."

Dorian snorted and kept examining Ledger's arm.

"Is this one of the bullet holes?" Ledger stuck a finger in one of the tooth punctures.

"Ledger!" Dorian and I both admonished him.

He hissed in pain. "Damn, that shit hurts. Lyss, babe, where are you?"

I chuckled. "I'm right here."

He turned his face towards my voice and groaned. "Nope, if I move my head like that, I'm going to puke. Hey, do you think I would puke up bullets?"

Dorian rolled his eyes and kept working on cleaning out the wounds.

"Can you, like, swim above me, doll? I want to see your face."

"Sorry, Ledge, gravity is kind of a bitch on land."

He groaned sadly and turned his head towards me. "Fine, you're worth throwing up for. Like that snowman said."

"Pretty sure that's not quite what he said." I climbed onto the table just behind Ledger, lifted his head so I could slide under it, and rest it in my lap.

"There you are! Wow, you look like an angel. Doesn't she look like an angel, Dory?"

"You know I hate that name," Dorian said between gritted teeth.

"You don't mind it when Lyss calls you it."

Dorian glared at Ledger, then at me. "Look what you started."

"If you want to get technical, you're the one who really started it by calling me my full name." I smiled sweetly at him.

"Don't listen to him, Lyss. He's just mad that he's engaged, so he can't have anything with you."

Engaged? I let an engaged man watch and instruct me on my best solo orgasms and then almost threw away all my self-respect so I could ride his dick?

Dorian looked furious. Was what Ledger saying true?

"Pain meds," Dorian mumbled by way of explanation.

Pain meds, my ass. We'd discuss that later, right now we had to focus on Ledger.

I stroked Ledger's hair back from his forehead, and he closed his eyes.

"Sing me a song, doll. You sang for Jem, but you haven't sang for me."

I shook my head. "Maybe another time, Ledger. Just focus on resting right now."

His eyes popped back open. "Your voice will help me rest. Please?" He reached up to grab my hand with his uninjured one.

I put his hand down on his chest. I couldn't resist those puppy dog eyes he gave me. "If you promise to close your eyes and keep still so Dory can fix you up, I'll sing for you."

A huge smile curved his lips as his eyes closed once more. I started humming Cruella De-Vil since he seemed to be on a Disney kick.

"That's humming, that's not singing." He stuck his lower lip out in a pout.

My eyes darted to Dorian to make sure he wasn't watching me, but he was too intent on now stitching up the wounds on Ledger's arm to pay me any attention.

I took a deep breath and started singing "When You Wish Upon a Star" from Pinnochio. From there I sang songs from Aladdin, Tangled, Mulan, Frozen, and Cinderella. By that point, Ledger started snoring softly. I tried to move out from under him, but his eyebrows scrunched together and he reached for me again, so I stayed where I was, simply brushing his hair back.

Chapter 15

Lyss

Jem and Rook came back just as Dorian finished patching Ledger up. They were both soaking wet again, but managed to maintain their shorts this time. Did they go back into the ocean just after sharks and people attacked them? Were they insane?

Rook picked Ledger up and carried him to his room so he could rest. Dorian stretched his arms over his head and leaned back. I could hear popping as he moved side to side. I slid off the table and realized one of my legs was asleep from ankle to hip. What should have ended with me falling to the floor was prevented by Dorian catching me and holding me up.

All the sexual tension that I thought had disappeared once we were snapped back to reality came back full force. My hands pressed into his chest. His hands burned where they held my waist.

We both stared at each other, getting sucked back into our cloud of lust. Then Dorian cleared his throat and pushed me away.

I yelped, but Jem was already gathering me into his arms. Good to know Dorian hadn't been just throwing me on the floor.

"Rook, with me," Dorian said. The two of them started towards the training room downstairs.

"Just a minute!" I shook my leg to hurry along the pins and needles that were shooting through it as the blood flow returned.

Rook stopped to look at me, but Dorian kept walking until he realized Rook was no longer behind him. He rolled his eyes and sighed as he stopped to look at me, too.

"What is it, Amaryllis?" he asked, crossing his arms. Blood, Ledger's blood, was still streaked along his arms and torso.

"First, you need to wash off all that blood," I began.

"First," Dorian said mockingly. "Why do you always have a list when you talk? Do you just keep track of all our faults and annoyances until you can't stand it anymore?"

"Just yours," I said, overly sweet.

"Second, you're one to talk. You have just as much blood on you."

I looked down. Damn it, he was right. My shirt and shorts both had blood on them, along with my legs.

"Second," I bit out, glaring at Dorian. "Family meeting. After showers."

"You're not a part of this family, Amaryllis." Dorian smirked.

Not going to lie. That stung a little, especially after what had just transpired between Dorian and me that evening. The sting was soothed a bit when Dorian grunted from Rook smacking him upside the head.

"Thank you, Rook." I smiled adoringly at him before turning an icy stare back to Dorian. "House meeting. Ten minutes. Does that verbiage please you, Your Highness?"

Dorian just rolled his eyes again and didn't answer as he went to his room.

Jem helped me to my room, since my leg still felt weird.

"Are you doing okay?" he asked.

"Just dandy," I replied. So many questions were running through my head and I didn't even know where to start.

"Did anything happen with Dorian while we were gone? I swear, if he hurt you..."

I bit my lip. I wanted to forget what had happened, even though I knew I wouldn't be able to, but I couldn't share it with sweet, caring Jem. How mortifying would it be if they knew I had screamed Dorian's name while orgasming and we didn't even like each other? What would that make me? Just some horny groupie ready to hook up with any of them?

"Siren." Concern coated Jem's voice.

"Something happened," I admitted. "He didn't do anything wrong, but it's not something I'm ready to talk about just yet."

Jem's lips pressed together in a thin line, but he nodded and refrained from asking questions. Instead of being relieved, I just felt guilty.

He dropped me off at my door and asked if I would be okay before going to his room.

I jumped in the shower for the second time that day. I turned the water as hot as I could stand it and started scrubbing at my blood covered thighs with my soaped up loofah. When I was sure the blood was off my legs, I started on my hands and forearms. Anywhere Ledger had touched me, I scrubbed, trying to erase any evidence of his near-death experience off of me.

It took me until my nose started running to realize that I was crying. He could have died. A shark had attacked him and he was shot with a spear. Yet no one seemed overly concerned. Then Rook and Jem went back out there. What if something had happened to one or both of them? Who would have known? Who would have helped? I knew I was growing attached to these men, but I didn't realize just how much. Thinking of never hearing a silly pickup line from my flirtatious Ledger had me choking back a sob.

I was past my self allotted ten minutes by the time I finished crying, showering, and getting dressed. Rook and Jem were sitting on the couches in the living room when I came out. Jem had his head tipped back and was snoring quietly. Rook was hunched forward, his forearms resting on his knees, his hands balled into fists, as if what had happened was his fault. Dorian was nowhere to be seen.

"Where is he?" I growled. Normally I would have laughed at

least internally at the unintentional, gender-bent Batman impression, but I was on the verge of seeing red.

Rook finally looked up and noticed me.

"I'll go get him," he said.

"No." I held my hand out to stop him. "I'll get him."

I marched to Dorian's room and banged on the door.

"What?" he called lazily.

I threw open the door and stormed in. He was lying on his bed with just a towel wrapped around his waist.

He looked shocked when he saw me, but covered it quickly with a glare. "Offer has been rescinded, Amaryllis. Not sure if you noticed, but my best friend had a pretty close call and that's kind of a mood killer."

Vision officially red now. "I called a house meeting. Why aren't you out there?"

Dorian's laugh dripped with condescension. "Since when are you in charge? In case you forgot, Amaryllis, you work for me."

"I don't work for *you*, I work for the band," I shot back. It was weak but I wasn't going to let him think he owned me in any way whatsoever.

"Whatever helps you sleep at night." He stood from the bed and dropped his towel.

My eyes shot to the ceiling, and I turned around for good measure.

Dorian snickered. "Come on, flower. You were begging for this cock just a while ago."

"No, I wasn't. Get dressed or come out as you are. I don't really give a damn, but we're having a house meeting."

"Hey, Lyss."

I was almost out the door, but my heart almost stopped when he called me that. I looked over my shoulder at him, trying to keep my pissed off look on my face so he didn't know how much hearing my name from his mouth affected me. Thankfully, he had shorts on now because he was coming closer to me. Slow, smooth, predatory steps and I was the deer frozen in headlights.

"Next time you come into my room," he stopped, inches away from me, "I'll throw you on my bed and fuck you until you're screaming my name. And I won't stop until you can't scream it anymore."

I should slap him or, even better, knee him in his too-confident balls. But after tonight, I almost wanted to step out of his room and step back in just to see if he would actually follow through. There were more pressing matters, though, and I didn't think I could handle Dorian right now. So I just turned around and walked off.

Dorian wasn't too far behind me when I went back to the living room. Jem was awake now and rubbing his eyes. Dorian plopped down on the couch next to Rook and I swear he did an extra wide man spread just so I would look at his crotch.

"Let's get this started so we can get it finished," Dorian said.

I narrowed my eyes at him before eyeing the other two as well.

"I think I deserve some explanations."

"You're not being paid for explanations." He stood up and Rook grabbed his arm and pulled him back down without a word.

I smirked briefly before putting on my I-mean-business face again.

"I've ignored a lot of things. Your late night group swims, your tendency to lose swim trunks when you go swimming at night, your innate knowledge of sea creatures, all the secret talks that stop when I enter a room." Jem looked away and scratched the back of his neck. Rook remained alert and intent on what I was saying. Dorian was staring at the ceiling and practicing fingering techniques on his air guitar. Aw, hell, why did I think of fingering? I looked away from him quickly, before my mind could wander further.

I crossed my arms in what I hoped was a power pose. "I will not ignore what happened tonight."

I paused to see if any of the boys were going to speak up, but they didn't. Of course not. Why would they? That would make it easy for me.

"You talk about being open and honest." I honed in on Jem, knowing he'd be the easiest to break. "Was that just a line or were you serious?"

"You know I was serious, Lyss." He looked at Rook and Dorian for help. "There's just some things that are a bit... hard to explain."

"I've been here for months now." I sat down next to Jem, facing him and putting my hand on his knee. Was I being manipulative? Maybe, but I wasn't going to let them sweep this under the rug. "What do I have to prove that you can trust me?"

"Lyss, if it was just my secret, I'd tell you, but it's not." His eyes pleaded with me to understand.

I sighed and looked down at my hands. He respected my privacy when I asked him to. I should do the same.

"Okay, I understand." My voice was quiet. "I'm going to sleep in Ledger's room tonight to make sure he doesn't get a fever or something. I'll see you in the morning."

Chapter 16

Jem

As soon as Lyss left the room, I covered my face with my hands and groaned. I knew she would suspect something eventually. She wasn't dumb, and we had some pretty weird quirks. I dropped my hands and looked at Dorian.

"What? You upset that your little girlfriend yelled at you?"

I jumped up, ready to smack the smirk off his face. "She's right, you know? She's been living with us for months. She deserves to know," I said.

"Why? So she can hold it over our heads? Listen to yourself Jem. You want us to tell someone who makes their living posting stuff online that we're not human?" Dorian laughed. "You have got to be kidding me."

I ran my hands through my hair, gripping the ends and pulling. He was right, of course. We've been keeping our secret this long, and for good reason. We couldn't mess up now. Except Lyss wasn't just anyone. She wasn't some random fan girl or a reporter looking for a scoop to sell to the highest bidder. She was... Lyss. The girl that fit in with us perfectly, complimenting and seeing the best sides of each of us.

"You know she's special," I finally said.

"I know she's wormed her way pretty deep into our family." Dorian stood up and started pacing. "How are we going to tell her she can't come with us the next time we go home? How are we going to explain that we're not even the same species? They put people like us in cages, Jem."

"She wouldn't do that. You act like you hate her, but we all know you're full of shit. You're just upset because of Grace."

Dorian whirled on me. "Watch it, Jem."

"No, I'm sick of swimming near fish eggs around you when it comes to Lyss. Just because you can't have her, why punish her or the rest of us?"

Dorian came closer until we were inches apart. "Remember who's in charge here."

"Like you would let us forget it. Don't forget that you wouldn't be able to be here if it wasn't for us." There was a time that I never would have stood up to Dorian. I had always looked up to him and admired him. He used to be my hero. Now he was just being an asshole, just like Lyss said.

"We're not telling her. It's bad enough I let you guys bring her here, but we're not telling her." Dorian pushed past me, knocked his shoulder into mine, went into his room, and slammed the door.

"You can't agree with him." I looked at Rook, who was still sitting on the couch, his expression as neutral as ever.

"My job isn't to agree with him."

"So you would just give her up? You saw how she jumped in and helped tonight. You've seen how well she works with all of us. We can't just let her go because of some secret."

"It's not just some secret. It's not even just our lives." Rook stood and placed one large hand on my shoulder. "You know I feel as deeply about Lyss, but this isn't a decision we can make lightly." He squeezed my shoulder and went to his room, leaving me alone.

He was right. I knew he was right. That didn't make it any easier, though. I was the levelheaded one of the group. I was the one that made the pros and cons list before we came up here. The one that helped come up with the damn rules. I made sure Ledger didn't go too crazy, Rook relaxed a little more, and that Dorian kept his cool around people. I knew the risks, and I still came.

I just never planned on falling for someone while we were here.

Chapter 17

Lyss

I started out on the chair in Ledger's room. Twice I woke up in a panic and rushed to make sure he was still breathing, not fevering, or in dire pain. The third time I just laid down on the bed next to him, holding his hand to reassure myself he was fine.

Normally the sun woke me, but Ledger's room was facing a different way and had blackout curtains, so I had no idea what time it was until I checked my phone and realized I hadn't slept in that late the entire time I had been there. Ledger was still sound asleep, breathing deeply. I tiptoed out and headed for the kitchen.

The boys were playing video games. I mumbled a hello as I walked into the pantry for cereal. I poured myself a bowl and sat at the island alone, reading the reverse harem book I had started yesterday even though I wasn't feeling it as much today. Maybe it was too much to think it was possible.

The noise from the game cut off.

"What the hell?" Dorian asked. "I was winning that round!"

"We need to tell her," Rook said.

The spoon paused halfway to my mouth.

"No, you know why," Dorian said.

"I'm going to have to agree with Rook on this one, bro." Ledger came from around the corner and leaned against the wall, wincing as he held his side.

"Ledger, what are you doing up?" I jumped up and slid under his good arm to help him to the couch. "You should still be in bed," I admonished. I brushed his hair back, discreetly checking for a fever.

"Ah, doll, I knew you loved me." He wrapped his arm around me and pulled me to his side.

I felt him nuzzling the top of my head and I just held him gently, glad he was okay.

"I knew I smelled something sweet last night. Were you in my room, doll?"

I nodded my head against his chest. "I just wanted to make sure you were okay."

"She was there all night," Jem said.

Ledger squeezed me tightly and kissed the top of my head. "Thanks, doll," he whispered.

"We need to tell her," Rook said again.

That got my attention, and I sat up just enough to see the rest of the group.

"No." Dorian crossed his arms like a petulant child.

"Let's vote then," Ledger suggested. "Rook's a yes, I'm a hell yes. Dorian's a hard pass. Jem, where do you fall on this?"

Four sets of eyes turned to my quiet song writer.

He looked hard at Dorian, making me wonder if I missed something. "Obviously I'm on the yes side."

I stood up and walked over to Jem. I sat on his lap and kissed his cheek before getting up and moving to sit next to Rook to give him a brief hug.

"Injured man over here. Wanna help a guy out and kiss my boo boos?" Ledger asked.

I rolled my eyes with a smile and stayed with Rook, but blew Ledger a kiss.

"Well, I guess we should start," Jem said. He leaned forward on the couch and looked at me. "Obviously, the four of us are close, but there's more to it than just being friends."

I stayed quiet, not daring to interrupt and tell Jem to spit it out.

"I'm actually Dorian's cousin. Our moms are sisters."

That was new. I've never seen that mentioned anywhere online.

"Ledger is Dorian's trainer."

"And best friend," Ledger chimed in.

Yeah, that one was obvious.

"Rook is Dorian's bodyguard," Jem continued. He looked away from me to Dorian, as if to ask for permission to continue.

"Okay, are you going to explain what the big deal about Dorian is?" I asked, unable to stay quiet. "Why does he need a bodyguard, but the rest of you don't?"

"Go ahead and tell her," Dorian mumbled.

Jem took a deep breath and turned his attention back to me. "Dorian is a prince of Sulamer."

The room was quiet as I processed what Jem had just said.

"Prince of what now?" I asked.

"Sulamer," Jem repeated.

I stood and looked at all four of the guys' faces. Ledger still looked tired. Dorian frowned at the floor. Rook remained expressionless. Jem was the only one that looked concerned about what might be going through my head. I giggled, then I started laughing. Ledger, Rook, and Jem exchanged concerned glances.

"Nice one, guys," I said, wiping my eyes. "You played that off pretty well. I'm surprised you got Dorian to agree to this, although since all he had to do was sit there and pout, it wasn't that far a reach for him. How did you even come up with that name? It sounds French or something."

No one laughed. I gave them another minute to break through their facades, but when they didn't, my smile fell.

"I think you might need to explain some more." I sat down on the floor in the middle of the room.

"Sulamer is a city under the Atlantic ocean. It's about five hundred miles from the coast."

"You're telling me you live under the ocean?" I asked slowly. "Under the sea?"

"Yes." Rook nodded his head.

I looked at Ledger. "Is that why you're obsessed with The Little Mermaid?"

"Yup." He popped the 'p'. "Hot merbabe disobeying daddy because she wants a man? Easy lay right there."

"How do you get there? I've never heard of boats doing trips to the middle of the ocean to drop people off."

"We swim, Amaryllis." Dorian finally spoke up, sounding bored.

"You guys are ripped, but not enough to swim five hundred miles." I stood up and crossed my arms.

"We're not what you would call fully human." Jem drew out his words slowly.

"We're a little more amphibious," Ledger added.

"We're oceanids," Rook stated bluntly.

"Oceanids?" I began chewing on my thumbnail.

"The term you would be more familiar with is 'mermaid', or in our case, 'merman'." Jem rubbed his hands on his shorts. He looked so worried that I wanted to reassure him, but I was still confused as hell.

"This might help it seem a little more believable." Ledger groaned slightly as he pushed off the couch. I immediately went to him, worried he'd hurt himself.

"What are you doing?" I asked when he started peeling back the bandages taped around his arm.

He stayed silent as he unwound the gauze from his arm. Instead of revealing the torn up skin that was there last night, there were only some stitches Dorian had given him for the deeper marks. On perfectly smooth, healed skin.

"What the hell?" I touched his arm gingerly, still worried I'd hurt him.

"It's fine, doll," he reassured me. "Look, I can even do this." He grasped me under my arms and tried to lift me up before a pained look crossed his face. "Shit, forgot about the poisoned spear. Those take a little longer to heal."

I chuckled in a sort of panicked way. "Sit down before you hurt yourself even more."

He didn't even argue as he plopped down on the couch.

I had been living with mermen all this time? The late night swims. The obsession with dried seaweed, fish, and all the sushi. Swearing to Triton. It was all right there.

I shook my head as I thought about it. No wonder they wanted someone to show behind the scenes. They wanted, needed, to appear as normal, *as human*, as possible.

"Were you ever going to tell me?" I asked. I looked at the four of them. No, no, that was never part of the plan. I nodded my head. "I'm going to need a moment to process this."

I began walking to my room and heard them start whispering to each other.

"Fine," Dorian said angrily. "Amaryllis, wait up."

I stopped but didn't turn around. Dorian came to stand in front of me.

"I didn't take you as someone who ran away from things."

I narrowed my eyes as I looked up at him. "I'm not running away. I'm taking a minute to process that you guys are freaking *mythical creatures*!"

"If you can't hack it, you can always leave," he taunted. He crossed his arms over his chest.

My breath huffed out, and I flicked my wrist. "I'm not dealing with you right now, Dory." I walked around him.

"Wow, you must really be in shock. Is it from the revelation this morning or last night?"

My back went rigid. We both knew he wasn't talking about Ledger being injured, but our little voyeuristic escapade. Which reminded me...

I whirled around and stalked back towards him.

"Last night, you said Ledger was hallucinating from the pain meds, but aside from seeing a singing crustacean, was everything else true?"

Ledger had mentioned that Dorian was engaged while doped up. Another secret that just the two of us shared since I was sure Ledger remembered nothing that happened last night while on the table.

Dorian's eyes stayed steady on mine as he answered. "It's complicated."

I didn't realize what I was planning on doing until my palm was already stinging from slapping Dorian across the face. The crack it made was loud in the quiet room. His damn face didn't even move or change expression. Tears filled my eyes at the betrayal I felt. And the anger of allowing myself to have any feelings aside from animosity towards this man.

"Fuck you," I whispered. I turned on my heel and went to my room, slamming the door behind me.

* * *

Once I was in my room, I realized I couldn't fling myself onto the bed and cry into my pillows. The memory of Dorian watching and conducting my latest orgasm had tainted the sanctity of my room. I slammed the door to the balcony shut, grabbed the blankets and pillows from my bed, and went to my closet. Once I closed the door behind me, I let the tears fall.

So many emotions washed over me I didn't even know what to focus on. Worry and relief were still prevalent from Ledger's near miss last night. Shock at what they had just told me. More shock and a little wonder that there was another world beneath the sea that hadn't been discovered yet. Or at the very least, made public knowledge. Curiosity. So much curiosity. How did they get their legs to be on land? What color were their tails when they were in the sea? Could they only transform in the ocean or did they get a fin every time they showered? Could they choose when to transform or was it an urge that they got every so often? Did they look like the Harry Potter mermaids or more like Ariel? Questions kept going through my head and when I ran out of them, I came up with more, whether or not I thought they were really important. Anything to keep the most painful emotion from flaring up.

Betrayal. Rook had plenty of time to tell me the times we cooked together, laughing and flirting. My gentle giant could have let me in anytime. Ledger whisked me away for moments often enough that no one would have thought twice about him spiriting me away and spilling a secret. My flirtatious playboy, that I haven't seen with a girl since I moved in. My sweet Jem had ample time during our late night work sessions. He was the one preaching honesty, openness, and communication, yet he never bothered uttering a word to me. Then there was Dorian, my... no, he wasn't my anything. He was someone else's. And I wasn't sure which part of that hurt more.

I couldn't be completely upset, though. Just because I had no huge, life-altering secrets to hide, didn't mean I could be mad at them for hiding theirs. And theirs was a doozy. I still wasn't sure if I completely believed it myself, but I knew they wouldn't lie to me about something like this, even if I tried to blame them for it, and seeing how quickly Ledger's arm had healed was just undeniable proof that they were different. And Dorian was a prince? An engaged prince? As much as I hated to admit, I couldn't blame them for keeping it a secret, especially with how under the microscope their life was being musicians.

My tears were gone, and I had settled into a state of numbness. I couldn't change anything they had told me, so maybe I could just ignore it until I built up a better barrier around my heart since the three— *four*, I admitted to myself—had somehow wormed their ways past the one I had before. I thought about moving to my bed, but knew I wouldn't be able to lie there without feeling Dorian's eyes on me. Scorching me as they drank in every piece of bare skin I had had on display. Or hear his voice, telling me to say his name or calling me a good girl. Nope, there was no way I was lying on that bed again. The closet was going to be my new resting place.

There was a knock at my door, and I ignored it. Maybe they would think I was asleep and leave me alone. About thirty seconds later, whoever was there knocked again, a little louder. I rolled my eyes and crawled to my closet door to open it.

"What do you want?" I called out.

"Can I come in?"

Rook.

"Fine," I said with a sigh.

I stood up and came out of the closet as Rook came in from the hallway. He looked at me, then at the stripped bed, then at the closet.

"Don't ask," I mumbled. I crossed my arms and looked at the floor, my cheeks burning. If Dorian wanted to do the whole open dialogue and tell them what transpired, then fine, but I wasn't going to say it. Not yet anyway.

"How are you doing, guppy?" Rook asked.

I snorted out a laugh. "Guppy. That weird nickname makes even more sense now that I know you guys are..." I gestured to him up and down with my hand.

"Oceanids?" he supplied.

"Yeah, that." I looked down and dragged my toes across the carpet in a zigzag pattern. "Anyway, I'm fine. Great, actually. If that's all, I'm going to go back to my bed." I used my thumbs to point to the closet behind me.

"Your bed is in the closet now?" A corner of Rook's mouth quirked up.

"Yup." I popped the 'p' and kept looking at the ground.

I heard Rook move closer, then felt his large hand cup my chin gently and lift my face up.

"You've been crying." It wasn't a question. His jaw tensed.

"It's been a long twelve hours," I murmured.

"Do I need to hurt Dorian?"

I looked into his eyes now. He was deadly serious, his nostrils flaring as he took deep breaths out of his nose.

"But you're his bodyguard."

"I don't care what I am. If he hurt you, I'll hurt him."

I stared at him for a moment longer, contemplating. "What makes you think he did anything to hurt me?"

"You mean aside from the fact that he came out of your room with you last night? Yeah, it didn't escape my notice," he said when my cheeks reddened and I looked down again. "I don't care if he was there because you wanted him to be, but I do care if he did something he wasn't invited to do."

"It was—" How did I even explain what it was? "It wasn't something you need to hurt him over," I finished lamely.

"You're sure? Because there was also that gorgeous bitch slap you gave him just a bit ago." His lips quirked up again in amusement.

"Ledger let it slip that his freaking majesty was engaged last night. Dory told me he was just high from the pain meds."

Rook searched my face, as if looking for any tells of a lie. Finally, he nodded once and let go of my chin. Then he shocked me by wrapping his arms around me.

I returned his hug, my arms barely reaching around him enough to touch. He stroked a hand from the back of my head and down the length of my hair.

"Who's Ceto?" I asked quietly.

"She's one of the original sirens. Her followers think of her as a goddess."

"What were those people that attacked you guys?" I asked quietly. "The crustaceans?"

I felt more than heard Rook's chuckle. "Crataeisians. *Crah-tee-see-ans.* They're a group of oceanids that still worship Ceto."

"What did you do to piss them off?"

"Aside from being Sulamerian and not worshiping Ceto? Nothing."

We embraced silently for several minutes with Rook stroking my hair and me just breathing him in and burying my face in his chest.

"You think at all about what I said the other day?" Rook was the one to break the peaceful silence.

You don't get as close as we are without learning to share.

His words echoed through my head. I leaned back so I could crane my neck back to look up at Rook.

"I'm going to tell you the same thing I told Jem. I need you to be extremely clear about what you are meaning. Especially now with all this new stuff coming to light. None of these sly little remarks that leave me stressing about which explanation my head comes up with that I should believe."

"We like you, Lyss. We all do, even if Dorian is being a total asshole about it and won't admit it."

"I like you all too," I admitted. "And that's the problem. How is that fair of me? How do I decide which one to like more?"

"You don't decide, little guppy. That's what we're trying to tell you. We've all discussed it, and we are totally fine with you liking all of us and *being* with all of us, if that is what you decide to do."

My namesake move came to life as my mouth opened and closed.

"We *all* want you." Rook's voice was almost a growl and his hands settled on my hips. "Do you want all of us?"

I nodded. "I know it's selfish, but I do. I don't know if I can share you, though. Like I said, I'm selfish."

"You don't have to worry about sharing us. You're more than enough to keep all of us enthralled by only you." He leaned down and captured my lips with his.

Chapter 18

Rook

I kept my kisses gentle. She was so delicate and soft that I didn't want to hurt her. I licked along her lower lip before sucking it into my mouth and scraping it softly with my teeth. She groaned and wrapped her arms around my neck to bring herself closer. Her tongue tangled with mine and I growled at the ferocity of need I felt for her. I bent down and grabbed the back of her thighs and lifted her up. Her legs wrapped around my waist and she clung to me as I walked towards the bed.

Lyss squeezed her thighs to push herself up more and gasped when she rubbed herself against my erection. I stopped moving. Having her slide against me like that had felt so fucking good, but I didn't want to push her into anything she wasn't ready for. She did it again, this time a little slower and with a lot more intention.

"Lyss, you have to stop doing that," I said through gritted teeth. My face was buried in the crook of her neck right now and I lightly bit her.

She gasped and leaned her head back before rubbing against me again.

"Lyss." Her name came out as a growl. She was dancing on a very dangerous line right now.

"Yes, Rook?" She moved again, and I saw the little smirk on her lips.

I threw her onto the bed and her brown hair spread around her head like a halo and she pushed strands away from her face while I climbed onto the bed to settle between her legs. My hands rested on either side of her shoulders as I hovered over her. I leaned forward and kissed her again. One of my hands went to her hip and slid up and under her shirt as I kissed her.

Lyss whimpered softly as my lips began a path down her neck. She reached behind me, grabbed the back of my shirt, and pulled it over my head.

I sat back on my knees and pulled the shirt the rest of the way off, throwing it on the floor.

"Tell me stop," I said. She looked so fucking hot laid out on the bed with that sexy smile that I prayed she wouldn't. Whatever her answer, I would do what she asked, no matter how blue it left my balls.

Her reply was to pull her shirt off, toss it by mine, and unclip her bra.

"Only if you tell me to stop first," she whispered. She was holding the cups of the bra to her breasts. They were so close to being free, to being exposed, to being mine.

I shook my head. "Never."

Lyss tossed the bra aside and reached for me. I wrapped my arms around her and turned us on our sides so I could hold her without crushing her. We kissed while our hands traveled. I marveled at her soft, smooth skin. I loved how she arched into me when I got close to her breast, how she jumped and giggled when my touch was too soft along her waist.

Soon her small moans became mewling and her movements became more desperate. I laughed softly, pleased with the knowledge that I was pleasing her, even if not to her full extent.

I worked my way down her body, kissing everything on the way. Collar bones, shoulders, the crook of her elbow that caused her to suck in a breath. I kissed and licked around each breast, slowly working my way inwards. When I finally sucked one of her firm nipples into my mouth, she groaned and pulled my head closer.

My hands bunched the bed sheet. All the little sounds she made, gasps, moans, whines, were driving me crazy. I brought a hand up to play with her other nipple while I suckled on the one before switching.

Her hips undulated beneath me, making me harder than I ever had been before. It was so tempting to just rip off the rest of her clothes and plow into her. She deserved better than that, though. She deserved gentleness, softness, reverence. Everything I knew I wasn't capable of, but was willing to try for her.

I continued kissing down her body. Her stomach, wrists, belly button, fingers. I grabbed her bottoms as I got to her hips and pulled them down, my lips trailing behind. I kissed all down her leg before finally pulling off her bottoms completely and letting them drop to the floor.

Lyss reached for me, but I shook my head and took a moment to see her sprawled out naked before me. Holy Triton, she was beautiful.

I picked up her foot and rubbed my thumbs along the arch. She sighed and closed her eyes. I kissed her big toe and her leg jerked as she tried to pull it back, but I kept a firm hold on it.

"You're a goddess, Lyss. Let me worship you." I kept my eyes on hers as I kissed the arch of her foot, then ankle, and worked my way back up her leg.

Her breathing was heavy by the time I reached her inner thigh. I breathed in her scent and blew softly on her pussy lips. She sucked in a breath and pushed her hips towards me, but I had already moved to her other leg and was kissing my way down it.

She cried out in frustration and hit a fist against the bed. I couldn't help but chuckle at her expense. I went all the way down to her toes again before coming back up. This time when I reached her center, I spread her thighs wider, grabbed her hips, pulled until she was almost hanging off the bed, and dove in.

Lyss cried out, and I could feel her pulling at the sheet. I swirled my tongue, sucked on her clit, and circled her opening. As she climbed closer to her release, her moans became louder and her breathing more erratic. Her thighs tightened around my head and I put all of my attention on her clit. She yelled as she orgasmed. I couldn't help but smirk at her volume. The other guys probably heard it, and damn if that didn't make me smug.

I licked her through every last tremor. Her breathing was still shaky as I stood and looked down at her. Her hair was a glorious mess, her chest and cheeks were flushed. She looked exquisite. Her eyes opened, and it felt like she was looking into my soul.

"Rook," she whimpered. "I need you."

I reached down and rubbed from her clit to her opening, slipping a finger in. I rubbed the front of her vaginal wall, making her moan again.

"Condoms?" Fuck, I couldn't even form a full sentence at this point. I needed in her. I needed to feel her squeezing my cock while she made all those little noises again.

"My nightstand," she said breathily.

I rushed to the table next to her bed and opened the drawer. There was a silky pouch with something in it, and a box. I opened the box and found condoms and lube. Our girl was prepared. I grabbed a condom and the bottle of lube and rushed back to be between Lyss's legs again.

I stripped out of my clothes and put the condom and lube to the side of her.

"Scoot up, Lyss."

She pushed her way up the bed, and I followed her. Her legs spread wider as I settled between them. I leaned my head down to suckle her nipples again and my hand went back to her center. I slid

129

one finger in, then another. She was wet, but she was also tight, and I was afraid of hurting her.

I sat back up and opened the lube, dripping some onto my fingers. I put them back in her and stroked along the inside, coating her.

Lyss reached down and grabbed my cock. She pumped it once, twice, before swirling the palm of her hand around my tip, spreading the pre-cum that had been leaking out around.

I groaned and pushed into her hand. "Fuck, Lyss!"

I grabbed the condom, ripped it open, and slid it over my throbbing cock. I took a moment to calm my raging dick down. She had me so worked up and I didn't want to be a two-pump chump.

Lyss met my eyes and reached between us. She grabbed my dick and lined it up with her. I pushed in a bit before backing out, then pushed in a little deeper. She felt better than I had imagined. My breaths were shaky as I tried to hold myself together, but Lyss was done with waiting.

She wrapped her legs around my hips and pulled me into her.

We groaned in unison, and I started moving, slowly at first, in smooth strokes. Her eyes fluttered closed and her fingers dug into my shoulders. I began moving faster, harder. She gasped and her nails scratched at my arms as I shifted a little more forward. I moved my weight to one arm and reached up to play with her nipples. She tensed, foreshadowing her orgasm, and I covered her mouth with mine, just in time to capture her scream. I pumped my hips a few more times and buried my face in her hair as I finished inside her.

I rolled to my side and pulled her with me. Our breathing melded together as we slowly floated back down to reality. I slowly stroked up and down the dip of her waist as she snuggled against my chest.

Chapter 19

Lyss

After a couple minutes, Rook rolled off the bed and walked around towards the bathroom to dispose of the used condom. I curled on my side, facing away, a relaxed, content smile on my face. Rook scooped me up off the bed, making me yelp and cling to his neck, laughing when I realized what was happening. He carried me into the bathroom and reached into the shower to turn it on without putting me down.

I shrieked with laughter when the cold spray caught us briefly before Rook moved us out of the way. He looked down adoringly at me and kissed me. I brought a hand up to the back of his head as I kissed him back. When the water was warm, Rook stepped in and finally let me down. We took turns washing our hair and scrubbing each other's backs. Hands slid over sensitive areas as we got clean and kisses were shared.

When we got out, I wrapped a towel around me and went to the counter to spray some leave-in conditioner into my hair. Rook came up behind me and wrapped his arms around my waist. A towel wrapped around his hips, but even with that separation, it seemed more intimate than the amazing sex we just had.

"Now, do you believe me when I said that we all like you?" His low voice whispered into my ear.

I nodded hesitantly.

Rook took my shoulders and gently turned me around to face him. "Then what's bothering you, guppy?"

My hand went to his chest. "I really enjoyed what we just did. Like, really enjoyed it."

Rook smiled. "So did I."

"But, does that mean we're—that you and I—"

"Are together?"

"No," I shook my head. "I know people can have sex with no attachments."

His fingers tightened on my shoulders, and he frowned. "That's not what this was."

"No," I agreed. "But where does that leave the others?"

He breathed out a sigh of relief. What did he think I was going to say?

"I thought you were going to say it shouldn't have happened," Rook replied when I voiced my question.

"Not at all." I stood on my tiptoes and still had to pull his head down to kiss him.

"As for the others, I told you, they're fine with it. Are they going to be jealous?" His chuckle was a little evil. "Hell yeah, just like we were when Jem told us he kissed you first."

"You're sure?"

He ran a finger down the center of forehead, where I know I get wrinkles when I'm concerned, and down my nose. "I'm positive, guppy. If you're really worried, we can go out and let them know what we just did and you can see what they have to say about it."

I clutched the towel tighter to my chest and shook my head. I was starting to be a little more comfortable with them talking about things as a group, but I just wasn't sure I was ready to be present for those conversations yet. I knew I couldn't do secrets, though, even if I just told one of them and he told the others.

"Um, you asked if anything happened with Dorian last night," I said, my cheeks warming.

"Did you lie to me earlier?"

I looked up at Rook and saw anger simmering in his eyes. I wasn't worried at all though since I knew it wasn't directed at me, but at Dorian.

"No, it wasn't anything that I didn't agree to," I quickly confirmed.

He nodded at me to go on, relaxing a little, but not completely.

"Well, after you guys left for your swim, I was feeling a bit, um," I looked down and played with my towel. Rook's finger slid under my chin and tilted my head up.

"You were feeling what?"

"Jem talked to me about sharing too, when he came to tell me you all were leaving. I started thinking about what he said and what you said and being with more than just one of you..."

"And it turned you on." Rook's voice was rough and his eyes darkened with desire.

I nodded. "So I took matters into my hands with my trusty vibrator. I had opened the door to the balcony so I could watch and listen to the storm, and Dorian saw me."

One of Rook's hands moved down to my hip, and the other tangled in my hair. "He watched you masturbate?"

Why did that word always sound so taboo? I nodded my head and looked down again, but Rook just tightened his grip on my hair and pulled it down so it forced me to look up. His other hand pulled my hips closer to his and I could feel him getting hard again.

"Did you know he was there?"

"Not at first."

"Did you let him keep watching when you realized he was there?"

I tried to nod my head, but I couldn't with Rook's hold on my hair, so I whispered my answer instead. "Yes."

Rook moaned. "How many times did you come with him watching you?"

My hand went up to his chest. "Three. I think. Maybe four?"

Rook leaned his head back and moaned. "Fuck, Lyss, that is so hot."

"You're not upset?" He had told me they wouldn't get upset, but Dorian and I weren't on the best of terms, not to mention he was engaged, so they couldn't really expect him to be part of the dynamic, could they?

"I'm envious as hell that he got to watch you touch yourself, but I'm not mad. I told you, we all agreed to this. Besides," he leaned down to kiss my lips. "I think I got the better end of the deal as far as firsts with you go."

He really wasn't upset. Would Ledger and Jem act the same way? I had talked to Jem about the idea last night, but I didn't know first-hand where Ledger stood on the whole situation. And Dorian just didn't seem the type to share, but he had a freaking *fiancée*, so it didn't really matter if he was or not. He was taken by someone else.

I was lost in my thoughts, only brought back when Rook smacked my butt.

"Come on, gorgeous. I'll make you some actual food. That cereal crap will not cut it and I worked up quite an appetite." His eyes looked me up and down, letting me know that the appetite he was referring to wasn't only related to his stomach.

As tempted as I was to feed the latter appetite, my stomach chose that moment to growl loudly.

"Yeah, food sounds like a good idea." I rubbed my stomach and went to my closet to change.

The other guys were gone when Rook and I came out. I let out a little breath of relief. I still felt raw and exposed, only now it was also physically and not just emotionally.

Rook threw together some sandwiches for us while I got out some chips and sodas. We ate together in silence, but it was a comfortable one. Our legs pressed against each other and Rook rested the hand nearest me on my thigh. He kept stealing glances at me, and I took extra care that there was nothing in my teeth each time I took a bite of my sandwich.

When we were done, I put our plates in the dishwasher and wiped down the counters while Rook put away the chips and threw the soda cans into the recycling. They were super big on recycling and it made even more sense now. It was beyond pleasing the "save the turtle" girls, but more about protecting their home. Their home that was at the bottom of the ocean. In the Bermuda Triangle. I wondered how long it would be before I could think that without partly feeling that someone was going to say it was all a joke.

"Don't mind me. I'm not looking. Carry on with whatever it is you're doing." Ledger came in with a hand over his eyes, peeking between his fingers. His hand dropped when he saw us. "Damn. I was hoping you guys had moved the party out to the kitchen."

Rook walked over to him and smacked him upside the head.

"And you decided to come out and watch?" I asked. My cheeks were burning, knowing that Ledger knew what Rook and I had been doing. If he knew, Jem and Dorian also did. I know it was supposed to be okay and all, but it was going to take me some time to get used to it.

"Hell, yeah!" Ledger grabbed a leftover slice of pizza out of the fridge before hopping up on the counter. "This is a communal area. If something is happening out here, it's happening for everybody."

Rook reached out to smack him again, but Ledger jumped off the counter, laughing.

"I'm just kidding, doll." Ledger wrapped an arm around my shoulders and kissed the top of my head. "I would never do anything to make you uncomfortable. Although, I did have to go to my room for some alone time, because those noises you were making made it a little uncomfortable for me to have my pants on."

I buried my face in Ledger's side as my face burned, but I still couldn't resist laughing.

"You're going to make her uncomfortable."

I could almost feel the glare I knew Rook was shooting at Ledger.

"No, it's fine," I said. I pulled away from Ledger so I could look at both men. "I need to get used to it, right? If we're going to do... this." I used my finger to point in a wide circle.

"Damn straight. We keep everything out in the open. You can start by taking your top off and freeing the tatas." Ledger wiggled his eyebrows at me. I smacked his arm softly. The memory of him covered in blood was still too fresh to do much more than that.

"How much you want in the open is all up to you. If you want to walk around naked, none of us will complain. But if you want to keep things behind doors quiet and one-on-one, then we can do that, too." Rook rested his hand on my hip and put a finger under my chin to tilt my head up.

"Let's start slow and see where it goes," I suggested. I stood on my tiptoes and kissed his mouth.

Chapter 20

Lyss

The next evening, I ate my chocolate ice cream as Clara regaled us with her latest right swipe.

"We were telling random fun facts to each other about ourselves. Just stupid stuff, you know?" Clara ate some of her ice cream before continuing. "After dinner and bowling, which I thought was an odd choice, but it was fun." She shrugs her shoulders and scoops up more ice cream. "I tell him that a fun fact about me is that I don't have a gag reflex."

"Oh my hell, you did not," Julie leaned her head back on the couch.

Gia and I looked at each other and snickered. Clara never was one to hold back.

"Hell yeah, I did. He was being so sweet and courteous that I wanted to make sure he knew what was on the buffet." Clara gestured to herself.

"Did he take you up on the offer?" Gia asked.

Clara sighed and set down her bowl. I sat up in my seat, knowing the story was about to get interesting.

"He showed me his purity ring and said he was saving himself for marriage," Clara said.

We all burst out laughing. Julie even spit some ice cream across the room.

"I think that's the first time you've been turned down," Julie said, wiping her face.

"I didn't say I was turned down. Did you hear me say I was turned down?" Clara looked at me.

I shook my head. She didn't say those words, but isn't that what it means when a guy shows you his purity ring after you basically offer to suck his cock?

"He said he was saving himself for marriage, but since he was pretty sure I was 'The One', he was okay to fool around as long as there was no intercourse."

Julie, Gia, and I started laughing even harder than before.

"A guy saving himself for marriage thought you were the one?" Julie howled.

"Hey, I'm a good girl." Clara pretended to look offended before grinning like the devil. "I know how to make men call to a higher power."

We laughed so loud and long that the apartment next to us banged on the wall, telling us to shut up. I wiped tears from my eyes and Gia climbed back onto her chair that she had fallen off of from laughing so hard.

"Did you take him up on his offer?" I asked.

"Hell no! I told him fooling around was perfect because I was on my period and too bloated for sex. Then I asked if he was okay sixty-nineing." Clara's smile was a bit wicked.

We dissolved into laughter again, shushing each other so our neighbor didn't get pissed and call the cops on us for being too loud again. It had happened more than once.

"He turned green and said that it must be a sign for us to abstain. He drove me home and asked for another date. I had to decline politely, unfortunately," Clara said.

"Don't they have dating apps for people like that?" Julie asked.

"Right? The one I use is for wham, bam, thank you ma'am dates. Not to find your soul mate." Clara shook her head. "I'll just never get some people."

"Lyss, you've been pretty quiet tonight," Julie said. "What's new in your glamorous life?"

I shook my head. "Nothing."

"Now we know you're lying. If there was nothing exciting or juicy, you would at least complain about Dorian," Gia said.

"How you can live with those four guys and not be having orgies every night is beyond me," Clara said with a wistful sigh.

I stirred my now melted ice cream and didn't say anything.

"What? Which one? When? Was it more than one?" Clara jumped out of her chair, kneeled in front of me, and grabbed my face.

My eyes went wide, and I stared at her as she squished my face like she was trying to make me look like a fish. I shook my head to deny anything.

"Oh, no, you don't," Gia said. "Clara's sexdar is ringing, and it took you way too long to deny anything. Spill."

I looked at Julie for help, but she just leaned further forward in her seat expectantly.

A sigh escaped me and I pushed Clara back. She let go of my face and sat on the floor, bouncing impatiently. I wasn't getting out of this. Normally, I had no problem sharing my exploits, but this was different. I had sex with one guy, but liked more than one. What would my friends think of me?

"I had sex with Rook yesterday."

It was silent for a minute before the girls started screaming. There were another loud couple of bangs from the wall before they settled down.

"I didn't expect you to hook up with him."

"What was it like? Was he rough?"

"Are you guys dating?"

139

Their questions and comments overlapped each other, and I held up my hands and laughed. "Whoa, one thing at a time."

Gia was the first one to speak next. "Are you guys dating?"

I pursed my lips as I thought about it. Were we dating? I knew it wasn't just a quickie fuck, but was it a relationship?

"I'm not sure," I said slowly. "I think so?"

"What was it like?" Clara popped onto her knees again and put her hands on my chair. Her eyes were wide and her smile leaning towards maniacal. "Was he rough? Did he tie you down? Did he spank you?"

"What the hell, Clara?" I laughed and pushed her back down. "It was amazing. He was gentle. He didn't tie me down. And he didn't spank me."

"Oh." Her lower lip popped out in an exaggerated pout. "He looks like he would be a rough daddy type."

I rolled my eyes and shook my head while I laughed. "Sorry to disappoint you."

Clara shrugged. "Eh, no biggie." Her eyes got wide. "Was he a biggie?"

"Down, girl," Gia told her.

"I didn't expect you to hook up with him," Julie repeated her comment. "You haven't mentioned him much before."

I pulled my legs up and crossed them. "Our relationship isn't stuff that would be brought up in normal conversation. I bring up Jem because of his book or play recommendations. Ledger for his crazy antics."

"Dorian because he's an asshole," Gia added.

I fought hard to keep my face passive as I nodded. No way was I going to share how mine and Dorian's relationship, or whatever we had going on, had progressed.

"Rook's quiet, but attentive. We make breakfast together almost every morning. Some days we don't talk at all, some days we do. Usually it's me rambling and him listening, but it works. He's excellent to snuggle with while watching movies. Best of all, he doesn't put up with Dorian's crap when he's a smart ass to me." I giggled. "I can't tell you how many times he's knocked Dory upside the head when he's being an asshole."

Which was even more impressive now that I knew their secret and their connections to each other.

"We need to have the next girls' night over there so I can land Jem," Clara sighed.

I forced a laugh. No way in hell. "Yeah, I'll have to see when we can do that."

"I have to head to work." Julie stood up and came over to give me a hug. "I'm glad you could come over tonight, Lyss. It's been a bit lonely without you."

"Hey." Clara smacked her on the butt.

Julie patted Clara on the head. "Love you, too, Clar-bear."

There was a knock at the door.

"That's for me," Clara said as she stood up. She gave me a hug and a cheek kiss. "Miss you, girly."

"Have fun," I told her as she hurried towards the door.

Gia got up to gather the spoons and bowls and took them to the kitchen. I pulled out my phone to check my emails. Julie came out a few minutes later, waved goodbye, and left.

I looked up from the email I was replying to when Gia plopped down next to me.

"Out with the rest."

"Rest of what?" I turned off my phone and set it down.

"The rest of the story." She crossed her arms and didn't break eye contact.

I puffed out my cheeks and blew out a breath. I should have known I wouldn't be able to keep a secret from Gia. When you're best friends since junior high, there's not much you don't learn about each other.

"I kissed Jem a few days ago," I admitted.

Gia's eyebrow raised, but she didn't say anything.

"And Dorian caught me in a, um, compromising position."

"With Jem or Rook?"

"With myself." My cheeks were burning now. So much for holding that secret in.

Gia snorted and sucked her lips in to hold back a smile. She nodded her head. "Okay, so that's three out of the four. Do any of them know about the other?"

"They all know about Jem because he told them. They all know about Rook because they were all home."

"And you're not known for being quiet."

I stuck my tongue out at her. "I told Rook about Dorian, but I don't think the other two know. Unless Dorian or Rook spilled the beans. They're super big on honesty and being open, which has been interesting, but good. I think."

"And they're all okay that you've kissed on and had sex with the other?"

I nodded. "They say they are. Rook and Jem have both said they're okay being in an open relationship with me."

"Look at you." Gia slapped my knee and gave me the 'get it, girl' look. "Two guys."

"Actually, when they said 'they', they meant all of them."

I watched as Gia processed what I told her.

"All of them?" She held up four fingers.

I nodded, then grabbed a pillow and buried my face in it. "I'm a total slut, aren't I?" The pillow muffled my words.

"Do you like them all?"

I finally looked up and nodded.

"They know and are good with it?"

I nodded again.

"Then, no, you're not a slut."

"But four guys?"

"Do we think Clara's a slut for sleeping with a new guy every weekend?" Gia pointed to the door.

"Of course we do."

Gia gave me a withering look.

I rolled my eyes and shook my head. "No, not really. She just likes the catch and chase game and sex."

"Exactly. So why would you be a slut for liking four guys that like you back and are okay with the situation?" she asked.

I shrugged and hugged the pillow to my chest. "I don't know. It just seems selfish or something."

"Amaryllis Lynn."

I glared at her for using my hated full name, but waited for her to continue.

"You are a grown-ass adult, as are they. If you guys want to be in some sort of kinky relationship where they shower you with orgasms and dicks, who cares what other people think? And why the hell would you complain about it? The only ones that would say anything are jealous. But your girls," she pointed to herself and to Julie and Clara's rooms. "We have your back and will support you in whatever you do."

I dropped the pillow and leaned forward to wrap my arms around her.

"You're the best friend ever, you know that, right?" I asked.

"Hell yeah, I do." She squeezed me tightly. "You're my LFE."

I smiled. It was our abbreviation for Longest Friend Ever.

We pulled back from each other.

"You're not mad that I might, kinda, have a thing going on with Ledger."

Gia waved her hand at me and laughed. "About as mad as I would be at anyone else my celebrity crush was in a relationship with."

"You refused to listen to Taylor Swift for a year after she started dating Taylor Lautner."

"We were like thirteen or something. I was dramatic in my youth." She flipped her hair behind her shoulder.

"Yeah, in your youth," I teased.

"I think we can all agree that Clara is the one that holds the title of being dramatic."

I nodded my head in agreement. There was definitely no arguing with that.

"You keep saying four, is there another band member no one knows about?" Gia asked. The look she gave me said she knew there wasn't.

"No." I grimaced. "The fourth is exactly who you think it is."

"What changed?" she asked. "Besides him being a peeping tom."

I thought back to Dorian's hungry eyes as he directed me how to touch myself, his frustrations at being unable to stay away from me. His plea for one night. Then I remembered the shock of finding out he was a prince, and an engaged one at that. I couldn't reveal that to Gia, though. Telling me caused friction between the guys. I couldn't betray the trust they put in me, not even to my best friend.

"It's complicated," I said finally.

Gia looked at me, but didn't say more. I could tell she wanted to know, but I just couldn't tell her. Not yet anyway. Maybe someday I could.

I stayed for another hour before leaving. As much as I loved our other two roommates, it was nice to have some one-on-one time with Gia and share my newly-developed relationship with someone other than the guys.

"Keep me updated on your harem," Gia said as I left.

"As if you'd let me have a choice in the matter."

"Just stay safe. And protect yourself."

"Yes, Mom. I'll make sure they wrap it before they tap it." I rolled my eyes, but smiled at her overprotectiveness.

"That too, but I'm talking about your heart."

Her face was serious as she spoke, and I could see a hint of worry on it.

"I know you've gotten close to them the last few months, but Ledger has a history with girls. And whatever is going on between you and Dorian..." she trailed off. "Just make sure you're protecting your heart so it doesn't get broken."

"I will," I whispered. I gave her a hard hug, then left.

Chapter 21

Lyss

"Hey, siren, feel like coming out with us tonight?" Jem stood in front of my open door. It had been a couple of days since Rook and I slept together. I was still trying to get used to being in a multi-partner relationship and the guys were all being beyond patient with me and giving me my space.

I sat cross-legged on my bed with my laptop open in front of me. I moved my bed from the closet back to my actual bed after one night. My back and a hard floor did not mix well.

"Are you all going tonight?" I asked. They had continued their nightly trips out to sea after the attack, but this was the first time they'd invited me.

"Yeah, Ledger is all healed up and eager to get back into the water."

"Does that mean I'll get to see your, you know?" I looked down at his shorts.

"Doll, are you asking to see what equipment we're working with? We don't need to go out for that." Ledger appeared next to Jem and smirked at me.

A blush colored my cheeks. "No, I meant your fins or tail. Or whatever you guys call it."

Jem pushed a laughing Ledger away. "Tail works, and yeah, if you want to. Or if it weirds you out too much, we can stay in the water and you can just pretend we're swimming."

"I want to see," I said eagerly. I closed my laptop. "When are we going?"

"Whenever you're ready," Jem said.

"Wear a bikini," Ledger called from out of sight.

I hopped off my bed with a smile and closed the door so I could get changed.

I came out a few minutes later wearing my red polka dotted bikini and a kimono style cover. All four men were sitting on the couches waiting for me.

Dorian's eyes locked on mine before looking me up and down slowly. My toes curled into the carpet under his intense gaze and I fought mixed feelings of excitement and annoyance. I forced my eyes away from him and his naked torso and settled on the naked torsos that actually liked me and weren't taken by someone else.

"Ready!" I announced, as if they couldn't tell.

They got up and we went out the back door. There was a pier from the backyard that provided their very own private entrance to the ocean. We got onto the boat that was docked there. Dorian started up the engine and we took off.

Things between the two of us were strained since the night I almost gave into him. We still bantered and snarked at each other, but it was half-hearted. It was kind of hard to pretend I didn't like someone I came for multiple times. Especially when he told me all he was doing was trying to push me away. Now that I knew he had a fiancée, it made more sense, but it didn't make it any easier.

Dorian piloted the boat out for about twenty minutes before stopping it. It was eerily quiet when he cut the engine. The moon and stars provided the only light in the dark night. There was much less light pollution out here.

"Come in whenever you're ready," Jem said. "We'll be close to the surface, so if you need one of us, just yell."

I nodded my head and wrapped my cover up tighter around myself. I was finally going to get to see their true forms. Would there be lights or bubbles when they transformed? Did it hurt them?

One by one, they dropped their shorts and jumped into the water from the back of the boat. They all disappeared under the water and I looked over the edge of the boat, looking for them. Just as I started to get worried, Ledger's head popped up with a wide smile next to the boat. I shrieked and jumped back. There were scales on his face. They started at his hairline and became less dense as they moved down his forehead. They looked like they might be green, but it was hard to tell from the quick glance I got.

Ledger laughed. "Come on, doll. The water's great." He floated on his back and splashed me with his tail.

With his freaking tail. An honest-to-goodness tail. Hearing it was one thing, but seeing it was amazing.

I threw my cover-up off and made my way to the back of the boat. I dipped my foot into the water and shivered. It was cold this far from shore. And who knew what was swimming around out here? I nibbled on my thumbnail as I debated how strong my desire was to get in.

Jem broke the surface a few feet from me and swam towards the boat. The water seemed to part for him, barely rippling. Reddish scales decorated his face. It should be weird seeing them like this, but it made them even more captivating.

"Are you coming in, siren?"

"I'm still debating."

Jem held a hand out to me. There were scales there, too.

"I won't let anything happen to you," he promised.

My cheeks puffed out as I blew a breath. I could do this. There was no gently sloping beach to ease my way in, so the best thing to do would be to just dive in. I motioned for Jem to move back, then jumped in.

"Holy fish balls, this is cold," I said as soon as my head popped out of the water.

Jem laughed and swam towards me. He stopped before he got too close and held out his hand again, giving me the chance to come to him when I was ready. He was always so cautious and took every chance to make sure I was comfortable.

I swam to him in just a couple of strokes. His arms wrapped around me and I wrapped my legs around his waist, sighing at the warmth from his body.

I couldn't be this close to him and not kiss him. He returned the kiss, caressing my lips with his. A large hand gently touched my waist, and I put my hand on top of it, threading my fingers through Rook's. I pulled him closer until he was pressed against my back.

They all had been so patient the last few days. Even knowing they were all okay with it, I was still a little nervous that I wanted too much from them and was unable to give enough.

"I've missed your lips," Jem whispered on a moan, leaning his forehead against mine.

"I know the feeling." I traced his lips with my finger, gasping slightly when he sucked it into his mouth and swirled his tongue around it.

Rook moved my wet hair to one side and started kissing the back of my neck. I leaned back against his shoulder and closed my eyes. A girl could get used to being sandwiched between two men. I used Jem's waist for leverage and moved my hips against both of them, and they both groaned. I felt empowered, confident, and horny as hell.

"Don't forget what happened the last time you rubbed against me like that," Rook rumbled. I shivered at his lips tickling the shell of my ear. I moved again before turning around to look him dead in the eyes.

"I haven't."

Rook leaned his head back and closed his eyes tightly. "I'm going for a swim before you push me too far."

He swam off, and I took the time to really look at Jem. The

reddish scales started at his hairline and trailed down to his temples before sprinkling down to his jaw. Little slits were along each side of his neck.

"Are those gills?" I asked.

"Yeah. Need something to help us breathe underwater." He smiled teasingly.

"Can I touch you?" I reached a hand out hesitantly.

"Siren, you can do whatever you want to me." He came closer to me. His movement barely even causing the water to ripple.

I put my hand on his cheekbone and slid it down along his scales to his jaw. "Wow, it's..." I tried to come up with a word that didn't sound offensive.

"Slimy," Jem said with a laugh. "Like regular fish, our scales secrete mucus. It helps us be more hydrodynamic."

I nodded my head. "Where else do you have scales?"

He held an arm up out of the water. Scales covered the back of his hand. They moved up, spacing further and further apart until there was just a scattering at his elbow. His fingers, palm, and inside of his arm remained the same smooth skin.

"If you let go of me, I can show you my tail."

I unwrapped my legs from him and swirled my arms through the water slowly to keep myself afloat.

He leaned back until his body was floating on top of the water.

The scales matched the ones on his face and arms, but were bigger. His fin was larger than I expected, stretching nearly three feet wide. I sat down next to him. The scales on his bottom half covered him up to his hips then quickly thinned out to a sprinkling just past his belly button.

"Whoa," I mumbled. "You're really a mermaid."

"Oceanid," Jem corrected.

"Right, sorry." I couldn't look away from his tail. The stars reflected off it, making it almost shimmer in the night.

"You can touch it if you want," Jem said.

I started with one near his belly button and slid my hand down

149

slowly. The contrast between skin and scales was interesting. His skin was still warm, but the scales were cool. My hand kept moving down slowly until Jem grabbed my wrist. I looked up at him and noticed the strained look on his face.

"Parts of the anatomy are still the same, even if it looks like it's in fish form."

I looked down at where my hand was. Flipping hell, I almost ran my hand over his dick. At least where his dick would have been if it had two legs to be between. All I could see were scales.

"Where is it?" I asked.

I heard Ledger laugh behind me. "Wow, doll, way to emasculate a man."

I covered my face in mortification as the boys all laughed. Rook was right behind Ledger and was laughing just as hard.

"That is not at all what I meant, Jem." I looked at him with pleading eyes. "I'm sure your penis is huge. I mean, normal." My eyes moved down and looked at the scales covering the lower half of his body. "Well, whatever it should be for a mermaid."

That had Ledger and Rook roaring with laughter again.

"Oceanid," Jem reminded me with a smirk.

"Right." I smacked my forehead with my palm.

"And yes, doll, his *penis* is huge. So huge that you shouldn't ever have sex with him," Ledger said.

Jem leaned forward and smacked him. "Are we done discussing my cock?"

I nodded my head vehemently. "Yup, yes, we're done. Moving on!" I turned my attention to Ledger and Rook. Their scale patterns were like Jem's, but where Jem's were red, Ledger's were green and Rook's were black. They flipped their fins up and down lazily. I scooted closer to Rook and touched the scales just above his fin. I looked up to make sure I wasn't touching anything inappropriate. I didn't think I was, but what did I know? He just watched me, not an ounce of worry on his face.

"Can you feel it when I touch you?" I asked.

Rook nodded his head. "Yes."

I touched the edge of his fin and jumped back when he jerked it towards him.

"Sorry, it's ticklish," he mumbled.

I laughed and looked at the three of them.

"This is amazing. You guys are real life merm—I mean, oceanids."

"Did you think we lied to you?" Ledger asked.

I shrugged my shoulders. "Not really, but seeing it in person is just a whole other level. Do you guys need the ocean to survive? How long can you go without transforming? Do you turn into ocean foam when you die? Do the girls lay eggs or are you guys still considered mammals? How deep can you swim?"

"Whoa, whoa, little guppy." Rook hooked an arm around my waist and pulled me towards him. "How about we have some fun then we answer questions back at the house?"

I agreed with that. We made our way further out to where the guys could freely move their tails around in the water. Ledger grabbed my arm and pulled me behind, instructing me to wrap my arms around his neck.

"Hold on tight, spider monkey."

My arms tightened in surprise. "Did you just quote *Twilight*?"

He winked at me and kicked his tail.

I rode in an inner tube behind a boat before, so I've gone fast on the water, but this was so different. In the inner tube, you're bouncing on the waves produced by the boat. Riding behind Ledger, though, was like flying through the water. Some of it sprayed in my face, but I didn't care. I just laughed and ducked my head down, closer to Ledger's head.

Once he saw I was comfortable, he started swimming in zig zags and figure eights. I squealed and laughed as my body was whipped back and forth and occasionally dunked under.

Our house looked tiny from out here and the water was even colder than when I had first got in. I shivered and Ledger grabbed my legs, pulling me to the front of him before motioning for me to wrap them around his waist as he encircled my waist with his arms. I clung to his body heat and snuggled my head into the crook of his neck.

"Look up," he said.

I did as he instructed and gasped. Out here, the light pollution behind us and the endless darkness of the sea in front of us, the stars shined brighter than I'd ever seen before.

"It's beautiful," I said. "Look how bright the Big Dipper is." I pointed to one of the few constellations I actually knew.

We stayed out for a bit longer, holding each other and looking at the stars.

"Let's get you back," Ledger said. "Your teeth are chattering."

I clenched my teeth together to get them to stop, not noticing that they had indeed been clicking against each other.

Ledger twisted me around so I was holding onto his back again before swimming towards the boat.

Chapter 22

Lyss

Jem was already on the boat, waiting for us. Ledger took me to the back of the boat and Jem helped pull me up while Ledger transformed back into human.

My whole body was shaking. Jem had my cover up and wrapped it around my shoulders, but the sheer fabric did nothing to warm me. Thankfully, he wrapped his arms around me and I burrowed into his chest, sighing at the warmth for the second time that night.

I heard Ledger climb back in, but kept my eyes closed until I was sure he had his swim trunks on. The boat turned on and I looked around. Rook and Dorian weren't on board. Were we just going to leave them?

"They're fine, but we need to get you home," Jem said when I voiced my worry. "We forgot how cold it is out here for a human. Ledger will come back out and pick them up."

We were quiet the rest of the way home. I just stared at the stars, moon, and reflections in the water. Ledger pulled close to the dock so Jem and I could get off, then he took off to the sea once more.

Jem led me to his room, then to his bathroom. He turned on the shower, putting his hand in the water to test the heat.

"I can shower in mine," I chattered out.

Jem shook his head. "I want to make sure you're okay. I'll wait just outside the door if that makes you feel better."

I shook my head. "Stay with me, please."

"Anything you want, siren," he said softly.

I struggled to pull off my top, but since it was one with no ties or clasps, it just bunched and rolled my hair into it. With an amused grin, Jem helped me out of it before squatting down and helped me out of my bottoms. He slid his shorts off and led me to the shower.

I stood under the spray and hissed before relaxing into the heat. Jem stood close, but still gave me space, looking at me like I was the siren he claimed me to be and I had him under my spell.

My hand reached out for his to pull him closer to me. I needed him close. We stayed that way until the warmth from the water finally sank into my bones and I was no longer cold. Seeing him in his true form tonight had built another level of intimacy, of trust.

"I wish I had something to give to you," I finally mumbled against his chest.

"What do you mean?"

I looked up at him, my chin maintaining contact with his chest. "You guys shared something with me. I wish I had something to share with you."

Jem smiled and leaned down to kiss the tip of my nose. "Siren, you're giving us everything. You haven't hidden anything from us. How can you expect to give more?"

My shoulders lifted and dropped. "I don't know. Tonight just felt special, you know?"

"I know."

We held each other in silence again, letting the water drip down us and wash away the saltiness from the ocean.

"Jem?"

He looked down at me.

"Can I kiss you?"

He chuckled quietly. "That's something you never have to ask me."

"Good, then we're on the same page." I lifted myself onto my tiptoes as he leaned down and our mouths met.

What started as a simple kiss turned hungry quickly. Soon, I was panting and Jem's hands were wandering. He played with my nipples and I moaned into his mouth. He moaned as I reached between us to grasp his cock. I stroked up and down, loving the feel of him tensing underneath my hand. I pushed him against the wall before breaking our kiss and dropping to my knees.

He stared down at me, his mouth open and panting. I smiled sweetly before taking the head of his cock in my mouth. His hips jerked, and he gasped my name. I swirled my tongue around the tip before taking him deeper. I used my hand to pump his base while my mouth licked and sucked the top half.

"Lyss, I'm going to come," he warned.

I knew he was close, his body was tense and his breaths had been coming out in quick gasps. I kept going, pulling him further down my throat. He groaned his release, and I swallowed it down. I kept him going slowly in and out of my mouth until he shuddered and gently pushed my shoulders back. I stood up and grinned. His jaw was slack, and his chest was heaving up and down. Steam swirled around us as hot as our desire.

"My turn."

My eyes widened at the growl that came out of Jem. I squealed with laughter as he flipped the shower off and grabbed my hand to pull me into his room. He picked me up and threw me on the bed. My sweet, kind, patient Jem had an animalistic side to him, and I loved it.

He didn't kiss me first; he didn't play with my nipples or work his way down my body. He just spread my legs and swirled his tongue around my clit. I gasped and arched my back. He slipped a finger inside of me as he sucked on my clit. I was already hot for him, from sucking his cock, but he was pushing me high quickly.

His door opened and Ledger came in. "Hey Jem, I was thinking about that new song."

Our eyes locked, and I came against Jem's mouth while watching Ledger.

Ledger closed the door behind him. "Holy fuck, doll, that was hot."

My legs were still splayed wide, with Jem between them as I panted. I held out a hand towards Ledger and he was by my side in an instant. He leaned over without question when I pulled him down for a kiss. I wanted him. I needed him. Both of them.

"Did him watching turn you on, siren?" Jem asked.

I blushed, but nodded my head. Seeing the shock and hunger on Ledger's face is what had pushed me over the edge.

"Feel how wet she is," Jem said.

Ledger kept his eyes on mine, arching a brow to ask for permission. I nodded slightly and his hand moved down to my pussy. He slid a finger inside me, making me gasp. I mewled as he stroked up. My hips moved, asking for more.

"I don't think she's ready to be done yet, Jem," Ledger said.

"I agree."

"How much more do you want, doll?"

I looked at him, then at Jem, still panting as Ledger slipped another finger inside me and Jem slowly circled my clit with his thumb.

"All of it."

"Have you ever been with two guys?" Ledger asked.

"No." The word ended on a whine as Ledger withdrew his fingers.

"Looks I'll be taking both of your group sex v-cards then." Ledger pulled his shirt over his head and I looked down at Jem.

"It's a first for me too," he admitted.

"Are you okay with it? We don't have to if you don't want to." I leaned up on my elbows to look at him.

"No way in hell am I missing out if you're down for it," Jem said.

I smiled. "Then let's do this."

"This is going to be fun. You have lube in here?" Ledger asked Jem. He dropped his shorts and crawled onto the bed, hovering over me.

Jem got up and returned with lube and a couple of condoms. "Ready."

"We're ready, are you?" Ledger leaned down and scraped his teeth on the shell of my ear.

I moaned and grabbed for him. "Yes, yes, I'm ready."

"Jem, get up here and lay down so our girl can ride you."

I loved hearing him call me their girl. Almost as much as I loved Ledger taking charge.

There was the crinkling of foil as Jem put a condom on before he laid down next to me.

"Alright, doll, swing your leg over and get on top of him."

I followed Ledger's orders and was soon straddling Jem.

"Now sink down on him, nice and slow."

Ledger was behind me, reaching around to play with my nipples. I held eye contact with Jem as I slowly slid down him. His hands tightened on my thighs and he bit his lip. We both let out matching moans when I was fully seated.

"Shit, Lyss, you feel so fucking good." He rocked his hips up and I gasped and moaned. I rocked against him, loving how deep he felt in me.

"I need those lips." Ledger put a hand on my chin and turned me to the side so he could lean over and kiss me.

While we were kissing, I felt a finger rubbing around the rim of my asshole. I gasped at the foreign sensation, unsure if I liked it or not.

Jem kept moving his hips slowly and smoothly under me and felt amazing. Ledger kept kissing me and rubbing my asshole. It wasn't bad, but I still wasn't sure if it was good. When Ledger pulled back to put some lube on his finger, I stopped him.

"I don't know if I can take that—you—that way right now." I

ducked my head sheepishly. I hadn't meant to lead him on or anything and I didn't want him to be upset.

His hand cupped my chin and lifted it up so I was looking into his eyes.

"Don't you feel bad about feeling uncomfortable," he said. "We're here to make you feel good. We can do something else. You can just use your hand or I can stand to the side and watch. I can leave the room if it makes you feel more comfortable. We don't *have* to do anything."

His words melted the tension I was feeling. We could still do this. He wasn't mad.

"I might seem like I'm the one taking charge, but the control is all in your tiny, soft hands."

Jem had stopped moving and I looked at him. He nodded his head in agreement.

"Whatever you're comfortable, Lyss. Nothing more. We can stop right now if you want."

I smiled and put one hand on Jem's stomach and one on the back of Ledger's neck. "You guys are amazing, you know that?"

"Amazingly turned on." Ledger leaned forward to kiss me. "Now, tell us what you want."

I rocked my hips, making Jem moan.

"I'm going to switch positions real quick," I said.

Ledger moved back to give me room and I pulled off of Jem just long enough to turn around and sink back onto him.

"Can you stand on the bed in front of me?" I asked Ledger.

He was on the bed so quick that I had to hold back a snicker. I licked my lips as I admired his length bobbing in front of me. I looked up at him as I leaned forward to lick the underside of his dick. His head leaned back as he moaned and I wrapped my lips around him.

"Fuck, doll. I love seeing your lips around my cock," Ledger whispered.

I leaned forward, taking him deeper. My hair had fallen in my face and he brushed it back, gathering to hold it behind me.

A hand stroked along my back and I pushed my hips back, rocking against Jem. He grabbed onto my hips and started moving slowly. I matched my pace on Ledger to Jem's thrusts, speeding up as he did. Soon we were all panting and moaning.

"I'm getting close," Ledger said.

I smiled around his dick and swirled my tongue over the tip. A pop sounded as he pulled out of my mouth. I looked at him with a pout, making him chuckle.

"Can you lean back?" Ledger asked.

"How far?" I leaned back, resting my hands on either side of Jem's waist.

"That's good," Ledger said when I was reclined about half way from where I was before.

Jem stroked along the side of breasts before grabbing onto my nipples. I gasped and moaned, still watching Ledger to see what he was planning.

"Spread 'em so I'm not dry humping your hairy legs." Ledger laid a light smack on one of Jem's legs.

Without pausing his ministrations on my nipples, he spread his legs which made my spread mine further as well.

"Perfect." Ledger smiled like a cat that got the cream.

My head was telling me to be embarrassed with how exposed and spread open I was for him, but watching Ledger lick his lips, feeling Jem's hands on my nipples, and hearing his small moans behind me as moved in and out of me made me feel beautiful and turned on.

Just as I was about to ask Ledger to touch me, he laid on his stomach and licked my clit.

"Oh, fuck!" My head fell back as I lost myself in the sensations.

I started rocking against Jem, but that only made me pull away from Ledger. He grabbed onto my hips, keeping me in place so he could devour me. I longed to touch them, stroke them, feel them, but if I moved my hands, I wouldn't be able to hold myself up. I was at their complete mercy of how fast, slow, hard, or soft they went.

"How are you doing, Lyss?" Jem asked breathlessly.

"Good. So good," I answered in between pants. His fingers traced circles around my nipples, brushing them over occasionally. His hips rocked rhythmically. Ledger's licks were slow and firm as they circled around my clit.

"Do you want more?" Jem asked.

I looked down my body at Ledger and saw him looking up at me, waiting for my response too.

"Yes." I nodded my head.

"What do you say?"

This new, teasing side of Jem was unexpected, but hot. And I was ready to do anything to get past this plateau.

"Please! Please give me more. Harder. Faster." My voice was strained and I tried to move my body to emphasize my words.

Thankfully my pleas were answered. Ledger sealed his lips around my clit, sucking as his tongue moved back and forth. Jem pinched my nipples, rolling them between his fingers and fucked me harder.

I screamed as I climaxed. I grabbed at the sheets and held onto them as if they could keep me from floating away.

Jem's hips sped up before he let out a long groan.

Ledger licked my pussy lazily as I came down from the clouds.

"You okay, doll?" Ledger's smile was smug as he sat up.

I nodded my head in response and reached one arm out for him to help me sit up and crawl off of Jem.

Jem rolled off the bed and went to dispose of his condom while I laid on my stomach.

"Holy shit," I mumbled.

Ledger chuckled. "You up for one more?"

"Hmm?" I looked over my shoulder at him. He was rolling a condom on his still hard cock.

"On your hands and knees." He smacked my ass playfully.

I yelped and got into position.

Ledger grabbed my hips and guided me back until I was at the edge of the bed. He stuck a finger in me.

"You're so wet," he moaned.

"I place all the blame on you and Jem." I pushed back against him, amazed that my body still wanted more.

"We'll take it gladly." He pulled his finger out and I felt his cock take its place.

I moaned his name as he pushed into me.

"You feel amazing," he said softly. He stroked my back, hips, and legs as he moved in and out of me.

Jem came back in and crawled under the covers. He rested his hand behind his head and leaned back against the headboard with a satisfied smile.

"You look beautiful like this, siren," he said.

I looked up at him while I panted and reached for him.

"Nope." He shook his head. "It's his turn. I'm just going to enjoy the view."

"Am I not enough for you?" Ledger asked. "Let's fix that." He wrapped an arm around my waist and pulled me up so my back was leaning against his front.

"I'm going to get hard again," Jem mumbled. His eyes traveled over me and I could almost feel his stare caressing me.

"Stop your bitching," Ledger said. One hand came around to play with my nipples and one hand went between my legs.

Thank goodness he was holding me up, because I would have melted into a puddle as he stroked me. My body was still sensitive from the last two. I reached my hand back to tangle in his hair. He chuckled and kissed my neck, biting my shoulder softly.

Unlike when he licked me, he didn't take his time. He went straight for the edge and threw me over.

I tried to cover my mouth to muffle the sound as I came, but Ledger grabbed my hand and pulled it down.

"Nope, let them hear how much fun you're having," he grunted into my ear.

I fell forward again, resting on my elbows as Ledger chased his finish. He slipped out of me and retreated to the bathroom

The bed moved and then I was in Jem's arms.

"Fuck, you are something else, you know that?" Jem asked reverently as he looked at me. He laid me down next to where he had been laying and climbed in with me.

My body felt like liquid and I yawned big enough that my jaw cracked. Both boys laughed quietly as Ledger slipped into bed next to me.

I scooted closer to him so I could lay my head on his chest and his arm could wrap around my shoulders. Reaching back, I grabbed Jem's hand and pulled him until he was flush against my back again.

"Mine," I declared, snuggling into the two of them.

"Without a doubt," Jem whispered.

Snuggled between two of my men and my body satiated, I quickly fell asleep.

Chapter 23

Lyss

The guys took me out for nightly swims about once a week after that. They each took turns swimming with me, except for Dorian. Some nights, I would just stay on the boat and watch, especially as it got closer to November. I talked them into going out at dusk one day so I could really see what they looked like, what colors their scales were. Jem only agreed if I promised to wear a wetsuit, since it was getting so cold. I quickly agreed to that and went shopping with Ledger for one.

It was much easier to make out the colors of their scales in the fading sun. Jem's scales were a dark brownish-red that complimented his mahogany hair perfectly. Ledger's were moss green. I told him if he threw a purple bra on, he could be Ariel. The next time we went out, he stole one of my purple sports bras to wear while he swam. Rook's scales and fin were solid black, making him look like a lone shadow swimming around. I lost my shit when I saw Dorian's. He normally was the first to dive in and the last to board, but Jem and I ran into him while we were out swimming one time.

"Yours is the only tail I haven't seen, Dory," I said while treading water.

"Are you upset that I've seen yours and you haven't seen mine?" He asked with a smirk.

My eyes narrowed even as my heart rate sped up. "I highly doubt I'm missing much, but a low bar needs to be set by someone."

Instead of being offended, Dorian just smirked.

"Since you asked so nicely, Amaryllis." Dorian swam around me and brushed his tail against me. I shrieked and clung to Jem. Even after seeing them in their oceanid forms multiple times, the feeling of the scales still wigged me out. I looked at Dorian's tail as he pestered me and started laughing. It was blue. Not a dark blue, but a vibrant blue that reflected slightly gold in the light.

"You really are Dory!"

Dorian scowled as I dissolved into giggles. I began laughing so hard that I couldn't keep myself above water and Jem had to help hold me up.

"I understand why you get so butt hurt with that name now." I wiped at my eyes that were streaming with tears from laughing so hard.

"Does that mean you'll start using my actual name?"

"I don't know, will you?" I asked, batting my eyes at him.

His face was serious as he studied me for a minute, then he smiled at me. A genuine smile, no mocking or menace behind it. "No way in hell, Amaryllis."

"Right back at you, Dory."

Dorian dove under the water, splashing me with his tail as he did. Jem and I continued our time together, and I pretended, just for a little bit, that there was no animosity between me or any of the guys. And that every single one of them could be mine.

I sat on Rook's lap, wrapped up in a towel, blanket, and both of his arms wrapped around me.

"We have to leave soon," Ledger said, interrupting the silence.

"Where are we going this time?" I continued snuggling into Rook's chest.

"That's the problem. We're supposed to be going to Sulamer."

"What?" I sat up and looked at Ledger. "When?"

The guys all looked at each other before Ledger answered. "In a week."

"Oh." I leaned back against Rook. They were leaving? I was getting so used to our little routines that I forgot these guys had responsibilities beyond what happened in my world.

"It's Dorian's engagement party. We have to be there for it since he's one of the guests of honor," Jem said.

My heart sank. Dorian's engagement party. The reason the one oceanid in the group kept me at arm's length.

"Do you want me to keep an eye on the house? Or would you feel better if I moved back in with the girls while you're gone?" I tried to keep the disappointment out of my voice.

Jem looked at the helm, and I followed his eyes to Dorian's bare back. His shoulders were tense, and he stared straight ahead. Whether it was because he couldn't hear our conversation or he didn't want to be part of it, I wasn't sure.

"Actually, we were wondering if you might want to come with us." Jem rubbed the back of his neck and looked adorably nervous.

"How would that even work? Even with diving equipment, I'd only be able to breathe for like an hour or something."

"Don't worry, doll. We have our way. All you have to do is say the word." Ledger winked at me.

"So, what do you think?" Jem asked.

Go with them under the sea and see their home? Not have to be away from them? "Hell yeah, I want to go!"

The boat jerked sharply to the left and I fell off Rook's lap onto the floor. Dorian was already looking at me when I glared at him.

"Sorry, there was a buoy in the way." He didn't even try to make the lie sound believable.

"A buoy, my ass," I mumbled. Rook helped me back up, and I snuggled into him once more.

Why was Dorian being such a jerk about it? Wait, why did I even need to ask that? It was Dorian. Of course, he was going to be a jerk. He was my number one asshole. Scratch that. He wasn't *my* anything. He was just a guy who happened to be friends with the three guys I was currently seeing.

I looked over at Dorian's back, watching as he steered the boat. Then why did I still not feel complete?

Chapter 24

Ledger

Lyss wasn't in her bedroom when I went looking for her. Since finally agreeing to date us all, she had been playing musical beds. Sometimes she would be in her room in the mornings, but most of the time she was in one of our beds.

Since she wasn't in mine or hers, that left Jem's or Rook's. Maybe I'd find the three of them all in the same bed. I'd be a little bummed about missing out on the fun, but she hadn't asked for three of us at once yet. I should have called dibs on last night since I knew I'd be leaving, but I knew I needed a good night's rest for the long swim I had ahead of me.

It pissed Dorian off when we invited Lyss to his engagement party. He claimed it was because we needed to be focused on our work, not on her, but I knew the truth. Hell, we all did. He's the one that didn't want to be focused on her. No matter how hard he tried to hide it, we all knew he was just as in love with Lyss as we were.

I felt for him, though. It had to suck shark balls to have her so close, but know he couldn't have her. If we were better men, better friends, we wouldn't be dangling temptation in a curvy body and bedroom eyes right in front of him.

Thank fuck we were total dicks who got the girl.

Jem sprawled across his bed on his stomach, snoring loudly and alone. Guess Rook was the lucky bastard.

I went into his room and closed the door quietly behind me. Rook was on his back with one arm behind his head and one wrapped around our girl, who was sleeping on his shoulder.

Her mouth was open slightly as she breathed. She wasn't quite snoring, but it was close. Damn, she was beautiful. She would blush and hide behind her hair if I told her. It made me wonder what bastard had made her feel so insecure that she blushed over every little compliment we paid her. I didn't think too hard on it though, because it would just piss me off. Instead, I lifted the blanket and climbed into the bed, snuggling against her back.

I kissed the back of her neck and kneaded her hip with my hand. Her legs straightened as she stretched.

"You awake, doll?"

Lyss gave me a sleepy "mm-hmm" and turned towards me.

"What time is it?" she mumbled as she rolled into my waiting arms.

"It's four."

"In the morning?" She opened her eyes just enough to peek out. It was still dark out and Rook's curtains would have blocked any sunlight anyway.

"Yeah. I'm heading out on a little trip, but I couldn't leave without saying goodbye to you."

"Where are you going?"

"You don't think you're going to swim to Sulamer like this, do you?" I stroked down her bare leg and brought it up to wrap around my hip. Holy fuck, she was still naked.

"No, but, well, I guess I haven't thought much about it. Will you be gone long?"

"Just a few days." I cupped the back of her head and pulled her in for a kiss. Her hands stroked my chest as she kissed me back.

"You're making this whole leaving thing hard." I pushed my hips towards her so she would know exactly how hard it was.

She giggled quietly. "Is that a bad thing?"

"It is when I have to leave and don't have time to sink into your wet pussy." I kissed her neck, right where it met her shoulder, knowing it would make her squirm and moan.

"Why didn't you tell me you were leaving earlier?" she asked.

"Because you were a little preoccupied when I got back and if I don't leave now, Dorian is going to try coming with me and we can't have him risking himself like that."

Lyss stiffened against me. "This is a dangerous trip? And you think I'm okay risking you?"

My heart swelled hearing the worry and annoyance in her tone. I loved knowing that I affected her as much as she did me.

"I'll be fine. I'm trained for this kind of stuff. Dorian is more important than me, and we can't have him rushing off just so he can get away."

"He's not more important to me," Lyss said quietly.

Fuck, this girl knew all the right things to say. I got off the bed and scooped her into my arms. She squeaked as she clung to my neck and smothered a small giggle into my chest. I loved her willingness to just roll with whatever I threw at her. Or carried her to.

I carried Lyss into the en suite bathroom connected to Rook's room and closed the door behind us before I turned on the light. Lyss barely had time to squeeze her eyes shut before I dropped her legs down and pushed her against the door.

She shivered and squealed when her warm, bare skin touched the cool door. My hands roamed over her body, stroking her stomach, cupping her breasts, squeezing her ass. Her hands grabbed at my hair as she moaned into my mouth.

I turned us and walked her backwards until we hit the counter. I kissed her once more and grabbed her hips, twisting her so we were both facing the mirror. Her hair was still messed up from sleeping and whatever activities she had been doing before. I watched her succulent lips, swollen from my kisses, part as she panted slightly, staring at me through the mirror. Her nipples were hard and practically begging for me to touch them. The way she was bent over the counter slightly and pushing back against me made it look like she was ready for me to own her.

"Fuck, you are so gorgeous." I cupped her chin gently and moved her head slightly so she was looking at herself and not me. "Look how amazing you look."

Lyss nibbled at her lip self-consciously and reached a hand up to fix her hair, but I caught her wrist and put it back on the counter.

"You're not changing a damn thing about how you look right now, because you are fucking perfect."

Her eyes darkened as she looked over her shoulder at me. I leaned forward to capture her lips, stopping her once again when she tried to face me.

"No, no, no, doll. I'm in full control this time. You're all mine." I wrapped one arm around the front of her chest to turn her back towards the mirror and my other hand went between her legs.

Her hands reached up to hold on to my forearm. Gasps and moans filled the room as I stroked up and down her slit, spreading her wetness onto her clit.

"More."

Her voice was a breathy whisper and made my cock twitch. I couldn't wait to get inside of her, but I wasn't going to have my fun without her taking the first ride.

"More what?" I opened my eyes wide with faux innocence.

"More of you."

I withdrew my hand and stepped back, no longer touching her.

"Hands back on that counter, doll. I want you to stay like that for me." I put my hand between her shoulder blades and gave a gentle push. "Leaning over with your legs spread wide, waiting for me. If you're not in this position when I get back, then we're not finishing."

Lyss's eyes narrowed as she debated whether or not to challenge me, but in the end, she didn't move. I slipped out of the bathroom and grabbed a condom from Rook's nightstand before going back in and locking the door behind me.

She was still waiting. Legs wide for me, pussy glistening, breasts hanging.

"Good girl," I said with a slow smile. Her eyes widened and her breathing quickened. Oh shit, did I just unlock a new achievement? Seems like my girl likes to be praised.

Lyss licked her lips as she watched me slip the condom on. Her ass swayed enticingly as she waited. I grabbed her hips with both hands and my cock pressed against her opening. I held it there until she whimpered, then I slipped the tip in.

My head fell back with a moan. Holy Triton, she felt good. So tight, wet, and eager. I pulled back out and pushed in again. Slowly. Agonizingly. She whimpered when I pulled out once more and tried to push back on me, so I tightened my grip on her hips.

"Patience. You were being such a good girl. I'd hate to have to punish you for being greedy."

Lyss moaned, but stayed still. She was chewing on her lip, making it plumper with each antagonizing nibble. I so badly wanted to just shove into her and fuck her, but seeing how much she was enjoying it, I knew I had to finish what I started, even if it was torture for the both of us.

I resumed my slow entering and exiting, going deeper and deeper each time. I stroked her back as I did, telling her how beautiful she looked and what a good job she was doing. By the time I was fully in her, she was a gasping mess.

I leaned forward and pushed her hair to one side. I kissed her neck, then her ear, before whispering into it.

"You're so wet for me, aren't you? So ready for me to fuck you."

A moan was the only answer I got from her and the only one that I needed.

"You've been doing so well just standing here, doll. Let's get you off now." I pulled out again and slammed back into her. She gasped and moaned loudly. I kept moving, pumping in and out of her.

She started moving her hips to meet mine, and I slapped her ass. She looked over her shoulder at me in shock. I just smiled and rubbed the reddening spot as I continued thrusting.

"If you're a good girl the whole time, I'll let you finish. If not, then I'll be the only one finishing this morning."

"I'm sure I can find someone else to help me finish." Lyss bit her lip to hold back a moan, determined to gain the upper hand.

"I'm sure you could, but we both know you want to come all over my cock." I reached around the front of her and pinched her nipple. She couldn't hold back a moan that time.

"Yes, sir." She smirked at me as my cock went even harder, if that was possible. Hearing her call me that had me close. No matter how much I teased her about it, I would never leave her hanging just so I could get off, so I knew I had to get her going real quick.

I traced my hand down her stomach to her clit. I rubbed it in slow circles, going faster until I heard her breath quickening, then stayed at that pace.

Lyss was screaming my name in no time. I debated covering her mouth, so she didn't wake Rook, but then decided, fuck that. If he woke up to her screaming my name, well, that's just what happens sometimes, right?

Her legs were shaking from her orgasm, so I wrapped an arm around her hips as I finished pumping into her. I came with a loud groan and just held her for a minute while we both caught our breath. Lyss was still hanging onto the edge of the counter, just like I told her to.

I pulled out of her and threw away the used condom before taking hold of her wrists and pulling her free from her death grip on the counter. I wrapped my arms around her and held her to my chest, breathing in the floral scent of her hair.

"You'll be safe, right?" she asked.

"Of course I will be. I'll only be gone a few days. Try not to let these guys bore you to death while I'm gone."

She chuckled. "I'll try, but no promises."

I dipped my head down to rest my forehead against hers. "The only promise I want is that you'll be waiting for me when I get back."

Lyss wrapped her arms around my waist. "I already am."

Chapter 25

Lyss

"Shouldn't he be here by now?" I stood on my tiptoes, as if that could help me see further.

It was two in the morning and the four of us were waiting on the boat where the guys normally went out for their swims. We had been out there since midnight. Ledger had left three days earlier and was supposed to be back tonight. Or rather, this morning.

"Be patient, Amaryllis. He'll be here when he gets here," Dorian said with a sigh.

I stuck my tongue out at him, even though I knew he wouldn't see me since he was leaning back in the captain's chair with his eyes closed.

We waited silently for another half hour until we saw Ledger's blond head break the surface of the water about thirty yards out.

"There he is!" I pointed to where he was and bounced up and down.

He emerged from the water, stark naked, and pulled himself into the boat. I threw my arms around his neck and kissed him while he spun me in a circle.

"I've missed you, doll," he said, hugging me tightly.

"I missed you, too. So freaking much." I hated having no contact with him all this time. Not knowing if he was hurt, lost, or worse, was a worry I had never dealt with before.

Ledger laughed and wrapped the towel Jem handed him around his hips. "It was only three days."

"Three long days."

"Guess I'll have to make it up to you." He leaned down to kiss me again.

"Damn right you will," I murmured with a smile.

"Where's Morgana?" Dorian asked.

My head whipped towards Ledger. "Who's Morgana?"

After Ledger left, I asked Rook and Jem for more details, but they wouldn't tell me. It made me even more curious and I had been going nuts not knowing.

"Morgana's an old friend," Jem explained. "Nothing to worry about with her."

"Old? Is that how you boys view me?"

I whirled around at the melodic voice. Like Aphrodite from the clam, one of the most beautiful women I had ever seen slowly made her way out of the ocean. She didn't stumble or splash water like I did whenever I was climbing into the boat. Everything about her exuded grace. A strap of some sort of animal skin covered her breasts, but below her waist, she was completely naked.

Jem walked towards her and held out a robe for her to slip into. His eyes didn't slip to look down at her body once. That observation alone warmed my heart.

"Hello, boys. It's been a while." She went to each guy and kissed their cheeks. I ground my teeth together, so I didn't smack her stupidly perfect face for putting her lips on them. When she got to Dorian, he pulled her in for a hug. They talked quietly for a moment, just low enough that I couldn't hear.

"Things between them are completely platonic," Jem whispered into my ear. "She's decades older than us and just a good friend."

"I wasn't worried," I replied quickly. "I mean, even if there was something, I wouldn't care."

The amused looks on Jem's, Rook's, and Ledger's faces told me they didn't believe me one bit.

"And this little puffer fish must be Lyss." Morgana appeared in front of me. I hadn't even noticed her leaving Dorian's side.

"Puffer fish?" I gasped. Rook grabbed my arm before I could do anything.

"It's like the human equivalent of saying 'that cat has claws' or something. They appear small and harmless, but can protect themselves when needed."

"Oh." That calmed me down a little, but I still looked at Morgana warily.

"Did Ledger tell you about our run in with the Crataeisians?" Rook asked.

"Yes, he did." Morgana frowned. "They truly had sharks with them?"

"Yeah, it almost seemed to be listening to them, but I haven't heard of anyone actually being able to train sharks," Jem said.

"That's because they're impossible to train," Morgana said. "They're ruled strictly by their need to survive. They don't have the same capacity as an octopus or a seal to learn."

"They said 'Ceto *is* rising.' What does that mean?" Jem said.

Morgana appeared more alert and she stepped closer to Jem. "You're sure?"

"Positive."

"If that's the case, our worlds will be changing. Prepare for war, my boys."

I felt the guys crowd me as if they were waiting for an attack right now. My hands balled at my sides, but for a completely different reason. They weren't her boys; they were mine.

She looked me up and down with amusement. "I never thought someone would be able to entrance one of these boys, let alone all four."

"Three," I corrected, pointing to Jem, Ledger, and Rook.

She cocked her head and turned to Dorian. She laughed and even that was beautiful, which made me want to dislike her even more. "Sweet girl, if you'd just open your eyes—"

"Do you have what we asked for, Morgana?" Dorian interrupted gruffly.

She smirked at Dorian's interruption. "Of course. It's right here." From out of thin air, because I didn't want to think where else she could have held it, she revealed a small bottle and a necklace made up of thin rope and a shell. "It will only work if she has enough oceanid in her blood to complete the transfer."

Wait, what? What transfer was she talking about?

"Can you test her?" Dorian asked.

"Of course." Morgana held her hand out to me, palm up.

"Does someone want to fill me in?" I backed away from Morgana's outstretched hand.

"Morgana is the one that helped us unlock our magic to become human. She can help you unlock yours to become oceanid." Ledger bounced on the balls of his feet. "You could swim with us, visit Sulamer."

"This is where you went?" I asked, laughing nervously. "To see a sea witch named Morgana?"

"We weren't sure if she'd be able to do the spell, so we didn't want to get your hopes up," Jem said. His eyebrows were scrunched in concern. "We thought you'd be excited about it."

"Yeah, what's the problem?" Ledger looked confused.

I laughed nervously. "Seriously? Have you guys never heard of King Arthur?"

The four of them looked at each other and shrugged.

I rolled my eyes. "It's a story, a legend really, about a boy that pulls a sword from a stone. A great wizard named Merlin declared long ago that whomever pulled this sword, called Excalibur, from the stone, will be the next king of Camelot. Morgana is the one of the main bad guys. Depending on which version you read, she was

Arthur's half-sister, but that's not the point. The point is that Morgana was an evil witch!"

"I prefer the term 'enchantress'," Morgana said with an amused look.

Shit, I just called the beautiful, powerful, enchantress an evil witch. I hoped she couldn't turn me into a real puffer fish. That seemed worse than a frog.

"Sorry." I wrung my hands together. "This is—well, I just didn't expect this."

"You may not want to expect anything yet," Morgana said. "If you don't have enough oceanid in your blood, the potion won't work."

"And you can check for that?" I asked.

Morgana nodded her head once. "If you give me your hand, yes."

She held out her hand once more. I looked at the guys again and when none of them objected, I placed my hand in hers. She reached into her hair and pulled out a long spike, and used it to prick my finger.

"Ouch!" Reflex had me jerking my arm back, but she had a tight hold on my wrist. She watched my finger as the blood welled up on it, then while looking up at me through her lashes, she stuck my finger in her mouth and swirled her tongue around it.

She laughed when my jaw dropped, and I pulled my arm back. She closed her eyes, leaned her head back and held her arms open.

We stood silently as we waited for her to find what she was looking for.

Morgana's eyes opened, and she looked at me with a renewed interest. "She has oceanid blood. She will be able to complete the transformation."

I sighed in relief. Ledger laughed and high-fived Jem. Rook squeezed my shoulder gently. Dorian continued his strong, silent, I'm-a-jerk stance.

"She also has the blood of my people. Quite a bit, in fact."

Her words silenced everyone, and I looked around.

"You sure you didn't just bite your tongue while you were sucking on my finger or something?" I asked.

Morgana threw her head back and laughed. "I like you. Anyone that can deal with this group definitely has my respect, but to know that you are of my blood places you in special favor."

She took my hand again and put the bottle and necklace in my hand. "When you are ready to go into the sea, put the necklace on and then drink the bottle. It will trigger the magic that lies dormant in you to fuel the transformation."

"What does the necklace do?" I examined the small shell that had to only be an inch long that hung from the necklace.

"It's a hundred-eye cowrie shell. The hundred eyes help to magnify the small amount of magic in you to hold the oceanid form, though I doubt you'll need the help, my young enchantress." She put a hand on my shoulder. "Should you ever wish to know more about what we are and what we can do, these boys know where to find me, sister."

Enchantress? Sister? Was I a sea witch?

She slipped the robe off, letting it fall to the ground, and turned back toward the sea. We watched as she dove back in and disappeared from sight.

"What just happened?" I asked, breaking the silence.

Surprisingly, Dorian was the one to speak. "She said you're part siren."

Chapter 26

Dorian

"Humans and oceanids have had relations going way back. There are way more humans than you would expect with mixed blood. Especially those with ancestors that lived near the sea," Jem said.

We were all back at the house, sitting in the living room. Lyss was sandwiched between Ledger and Rook while Jem and I occupied the other couch.

"That makes sense, seeing as you guys are here walking around on two legs with perfectly functioning dicks." Lyss sipped a cup of hot chocolate and pulled her feet up to tuck underneath Rook's legs and lean against Ledger.

"I'm willing to prove how perfectly functioning mine still is." Ledger lifted his arm for her to cuddle into his side and rubbed her bare thigh. Damn guy hadn't stopped touching her since he got back. You'd think he was gone for three years, not just three lousy days. And he got to touch her just before he left. Her cries of pleasure had been my alarm clock that morning. I took a long shower to drown out the tempting sounds, and when I got out, I found out that Ledger had already left to find Morgana. Without me.

Lyss patted his hand. "Tonight, I promise. The adults are talking right now."

Rook snorted out a laugh and pulled one of her tan legs over his so he could rub her foot. She wiggled her purple-painted toes and sighed.

I bit my cheek to hold back from glaring at them all. I couldn't be mad. My best friends were happy and with someone who was pretty fucking awesome. Just because I was bitter that they got her, and I didn't wasn't reason enough to punish them. Although Poseidon knew I wanted to.

I was beyond livid when they invited her to my engagement party. Did they really expect me to play the doting fiancée when the girl that haunted my dreams and fueled my fantasies was swimming around? It was the worst kind of torture. Having something I wanted so bad so fucking close and being unable to do anything about it.

The guys knew I liked her, but even they didn't understand the spell she had me under. If they did, they would push her away out of solidarity, and that just wasn't fair for me to ask of them.

"You're just jealous because I get Lyss all to myself tonight." Ledger brought me back to the present as he taunted Rook. "You guys get to listen to me make her scream all night long."

"Stop it." Lyss batted at Ledger's hand half-heartedly as her cheeks flushed. Ledger just laughed and kissed the side of her face.

I groaned internally. I knew Ledger would make true on his words and I would hear Lyss's sweet voice moaning, whimpering, and screaming tonight. And just because I liked to fuck with my head, I would leave my door open so I could hear her better. Watching her that night only made it worse because I could picture the faces she would make and imagine how her body would writhe as she was touched.

"How many oceanids are on land right now?" Lyss asked.

"I'd say about four." Jem shrugged his shoulders.

Lyss looked at all of us, scrunching her eyebrows as she searched for a sign of Jem lying. "Are you telling me you four are the only oceanids on land right now?"

"Ooh, story time." Ledger clapped his hands and rubbed them together.

"Is everyone ready?" Jem asked dryly, arching a brow as he looked at Ledger. I smirked at his unamused look. Ledger was the biggest kid out of all of us and it sometimes drove my overly serious cousin nuts.

"Sirens are the originals. They are where the myth of mermaids began," Jem began.

"But they're not a myth," Lyss interrupted.

"To most of the world they are." Jem settled back against the couch as he got into his professor mode. "Sirens really would lure sailors to their death with their voices, but while that happened occasionally, most sirens would simply transform and come onto land to seduce men and escape back to the sea. They would carry the child to term and what happened next depended on how they were born. If the baby was born with a tail, they lived in the ocean to be raised by their mothers. If it was born with legs, they would be left on land for someone to, hopefully, find and be raised in the human world."

"Looks like some mothers got their skills from sirens," Lyss muttered. Her eyes focused on the floor, but her mind seemed to be in another place. It took her a minute to notice that Jem had stopped talking and was watching her. All of us were.

"Something you want to tell us, siren?" Jem asked.

Lyss shook her head, then sighed. "I'm adopted. Apparently, my womb donor just dumped me at a hospital. It was for the best, though, I guess. I couldn't ask for more amazing parents."

Her smile was forced, and I knew it hurt her more than she was letting on. Another new petal of our flower's story.

"Sirens can't be gone from the water for long. It's where they get their power," Rook continued, sensing Lyss's uncomfortableness. "If the baby was more human than oceanid, the only other option would be to let it drown."

Lyss's jaw dropped in horror. "When you put it that way, beach babies aren't such a horrible idea."

"Just like how you can have brown eyes but carry a recessive gene for blue eyes to pass down to your kids. It's the same with oceanids and humans. The exception is when a child receives a dominant human gene versus oceanid, they and their posterity will remain human unless they can wake their dormant gene. Same with oceanids," Jem said.

"How the hell do you know about recessive and dominant genes?" Lyss asked Jem.

"Because our little Jem here is a big nerd." Ledger got up and patted the top of Jem's head as he walked into the kitchen to make himself something.

"It's called increasing one's knowledge." Jem chucked a throw pillow at Ledger's back. "Also, because it's required teaching at school. Some of us actually paid attention."

"I never thought about you guys having schools down there," Lyss said, her brow furrowed.

"We're literally part fish. Of course, there are schools." Ledger said from the kitchen.

We all rolled our eyes at his lame joke.

"Ha ha. You know what I mean. I just didn't think of little oceanid kids getting up and going to school every morning like I did when I was little." Lyss looked at Jem, concerned. "They are still called kids, right? Not hatchlings or whatever baby fish are called?"

"Fry," Rook said.

"You fry what now?" Lyss asked.

"Newborn fish are called fry, Amaryllis," I said, rolling my eyes. "We don't fry up our kids."

Lyss glared at me. That was the only way I could stand her looking at me. As long as she kept her guard up around me, I could keep my distance.

"And hatchlings wouldn't be accurate because oceanids give birth to live babies, just like humans," Jem added.

183

"So what exactly should I expect while we're down there? I obviously have an extremely non-realistic view of what life is like for you guys down there."

"It's pretty similar to here, just under water and with a tail." Ledger plopped himself back down next to Lyss with his sandwich.

"Yeah, I'm sure it's just like living here with gravity, air pollution, sunburns, and vehicles." Lyss scoffed and rolled her eyes, but still smiled and leaned against Ledger.

"The difference in gravity and sunburns are a pretty big difference, but we still have to worry about pollution and we have different modes of transportation," Jem said.

Lyss cocked her head to the side. She opened her mouth to ask something, but a look of confusion crossed her face. "Wait, you said oceanids are like humans, but the oceanid gene is dominant, right? So their human genes are dormant?"

Jem nodded his head.

"How are you guys able to transform, then?"

"That would be thanks to the lovely Morgana. Don't worry, doll, you're still my number one." Ledger kissed the side of Lyss's head with his mouthful of sandwich.

"Sirens are magical. They're the mother of our species and there aren't many left. Morgana used to live in Sulamer. She had a shop there selling different potions and such." Jem leaned forward and rested his forearms on his knees.

"So she really is a sea witch." A smile lit up Lyss's face. "I was right."

The other three laughed, and even I had to bite my tongue to keep from joining. The proud smirk on her face was fucking adorable.

"Yes, little guppy, you were right. Just don't let her hear you call her that. As she said, she prefers the term enchantress. Witch has such a negative connotation, especially after those witch trials on land a few hundred years ago." Rook patted her leg and left his hand there, idly stroking it.

"Dorian snuck out of the castle often—"

"You live in a castle?" Lyss interrupted Jem and stared at me with wide eyes.

I scoffed as I stood. "Real life prince here, Amaryllis. Of course, I live in a fucking castle." I went to the kitchen and poured a glass of water. Even without seeing her, I could feel her eyes following me, burning into my back. I had my shirt off, ready for bed since it was so damn late, but I didn't want to leave the group. In all honesty, I didn't want to leave Lyss. The wonder on her face whenever we spoke of Sulamer was intoxicating. The excitement, the dreaminess she had of the place that was feeling more and more like a prison to me, was oddly refreshing. She was making me see the wonders of our world once again. The world seemed brighter through her eyes. Even the pictures she took and posted to our social media accounts were happier, clearer. I wanted that light, but I was made for darkness. I couldn't bring her into that, so the only thing I could do was push her away.

"Dorian would go to see Morgana for a potion that would essentially render him invisible," Jem continued.

"Did the poor little prince want to sneak into the kitchen without getting caught?" Lyss stuck her bottom lip out in a sarcastic pout. "Or were you trying to spy on people having sex?"

I grinned and wiped my mouth with the back of my hand. "I've found that people enjoy it more when they know I'm watching them. Wouldn't you agree, Amaryllis?"

She set herself up for that one and she knew it. She pursed her lips and turned her attention back to Jem.

"One night when Dorian snuck out to visit with her, he noticed the door to her shop hadn't been shut all the way. He heard her scream and when he went in, he found several males attacking Morgana."

"Come on, Jem, don't sugarcoat it for her." It still burned, remembering what I had walked in on those men doing to Morgana. I moved across the room until I was standing in front of her, then squatted down so I could look her in the eyes. "The bastards were raping her. They took turns holding her down and fucking her because she gave them a wrong potion. They wanted an alluring potion, but she knew why they really wanted it, so she gave them a repelling potion instead. When they figured it out, they waited until the shops were closed up for the night and everyone had left, broke in, and raped her."

Lyss's face had gone white. "Why didn't she just blast them with her magic or something?"

"It's hard to fight against five men when they ambush you." I chucked her chin. "Hate to spoil your view of Sulamer already, but it's not all friendly fish and singing crabs down there."

I stood and headed straight to the balcony. The door slammed behind me, and I gripped the railing and stared out into the water. I hadn't been able to help Morgana then. I had tried, but got the shit beat out of me. They left both Morgana and me broken on the floor. Her more so, yet she was the one to help me, to get the potions needed to help heal me. That was when I began taking my lessons with Ledger seriously. I wasn't ever going to be helpless again. For myself or for someone I cared about.

I heard the door click shut quietly. Only one person would close it that quietly and I couldn't deal with her right now. Not when I had just revealed how weak I was.

"You did the best you could." Her voice was quiet. I could only hear her because she stood right next to me. She had her folded arms on the railing, inches from my hand, and she stared out at the ocean instead of at me.

I smiled ruefully. "Don't try to placate me, Amaryllis. I could have done better. I should have done better."

"You did the best you could."

"You weren't even there. How would you know?"

"Because I know you. You helped her the best you could and even though you feel you failed, you're the reason she's still here."

I finally looked at her. Her face was so calm, so confident, as she continued to stare straight ahead.

"You don't know me, Amaryllis. All you see when you look at me is a royal asshole."

She smiled. "I'm not denying that, but I also know that for whatever reason, that royal asshole attitude is usually just directed towards me. You're a good man, Dorian. Even if you think you're not."

She still wasn't looking at me. I scooted closer and grabbed the railing on either side of her, boxing her in and pushing against her back.

"Get your head out of the clouds. Stop painting this fantasy you have of me and life under the sea. It's not bright colors, singing crustaceans, and happily ever-afters. It's dark and deadly. That is where I'm from. That is what I am."

Lyss twisted to face me, the peaceful smile still on her face. She looked up and put a hand on my cheek. My eyes widened at the gentle touch and complete look of trust in her eyes.

"Even if you don't show me that side of you, I know it because I've seen how you treat fans at events. I've seen how you treated my friends. And those three guys in there would give their lives for you in a heartbeat if needed, and I trust them. They're from the same dark place as you, yet they reached for the light, for you. So keep being my asshole, but I know there's more to you than what you show me."

Her hand slid slowly down my face, but I grabbed her wrist, stopping her from leaving me.

"Why do you make this so fucking difficult?" I growled. I was pissed, hopeful, and drowning in her hazel eyes. It was a potent combination, especially while inhaling the scent that was inherently Lyss.

Instead of answering with a smart remark, she kissed me. She stood on her tiptoes and placed her lips on mine. And I couldn't hold back any longer.

Chapter 27

Lyss

The sorrow, hurt, and blame in Dorian's eyes about broke me. Every word I said to him was true. I knew he was a good man. Even if he constantly pushed me away, needled me just to piss me off, I knew he had his reasons.

When I went out there, I had planned on just talking. I knew he would be grumpy and angry. What I didn't expect was to see the hunger in his eyes when he tried to intimidate me. The desperation of acceptance, the need to be understood. It was there, though, in my asshole prince. And mine he was, regardless of how we had been trying to avoid it.

It shocked him when I kissed him. He stood frozen as I pressed my lips to his. It was a soft kiss, and even with him practically unresponsive, it still sent shivers down my spine.

As I lowered from my tiptoes, he grabbed my hair and pulled on it, tilting my head up for better access. I bit his lip, causing him to groan and slap my ass. I yelped and smacked his chest. His lips vibrated against mine as he chuckled. He grabbed both my hands and pulled them behind me. My back arched against him. My nipples hardened when they rubbed against his chest as we fought for dominance, our lips never leaving each other. I stepped on his foot. An oomph left him and he let go of my hands, only to grab the back of my thighs and place me on the railing. My arms went around his neck. One hand pulled at his hair and the other grabbed at his shoulder, both pulling him closer.

Dorian stood back from me briefly to whip my shirt off, then was back on me. He grabbed behind my knees and tugged me into him, rubbing his hard dick against my center. I whimpered at the sensations the friction was sending through me. I locked my legs around him and scratched at his back, pulling him closer and punishing him at the same time.

His hands moved across my body. On my waist one minute, kneading my ass the next, rubbing the spot where my groin met my thigh. He held me as we stepped back and we continued our onslaught of each other as he carried me through the house.

"About fucking time," someone muttered.

My back was pushed against a door and Dorian let me down and took a step back. We were both breathing heavily as we looked at each other. His lip was red where I bit it and I could feel how swollen mine were. My nipples and pussy ached for his touch.

He leaned forward and opened the door behind me. It was to his room. I grabbed the waistband of his shorts and took a step back, stopping when he braced his arms on the door frame, looking at me like he had the night he watched me from the balcony.

"I told you that the next time you came into my room, I would throw you on that bed and fuck you until you couldn't scream my name anymore. Are you sure you're up for that?"

I arched a brow at him. "Only if you think you have the stamina to follow through."

His grin was full of promises that made me even wetter for him. I grinned back at him and tried pulling him into the room again, but he didn't move.

I groaned. "Really? You want to talk now? Are we going to do this or what, Dory?"

"One night." Dorian's eyes bore into mine. "That's all I can give you, Lyss. Just one night."

One night? Just one night with him? One night with this cocky, overbearing, grumpy, mythical asshole? I looked over my shoulder at his bed, large and inviting and still mussed from when he got up this morning. Then I looked back at him. His mask was back on, showing no emotion. He was waiting for me to turn him down. Knowing that he had to brace himself to prepare for my denial crumbled the rest of my defenses. I reached up and grabbed his face with both hands.

"If one night is all we get together, let's make it a fucking good one."

Dorian finally dropped his arms and walked through the door with me. He closed the door when we were in, covering us in darkness. Just enough light bled through the curtains so that we could see each other. We stared at each other silently, not touching, but close enough to feel the heat from each other and hear each other's labored breaths.

I stepped forward, putting my hand on his shoulder to pull him down to me, unable to stay away from him any longer. The spell was broken, and the intensity was back. Dorian pushed me back until my legs hit the bed, then he picked me up and threw me on it. Before I could brush the hair out of my face, he grabbed my bottoms and pulled them off. When I sat up, his shorts were gone too, and he stroked his erection as he stared at me.

"I'm keeping these." He held up my purple panties to show me before throwing them on top of his dresser. "Take off your bra."

"Make me," I taunted him.

He growled. "Now, Amaryllis."

With a smirk, I got onto my knees. I pushed one strap down slowly before sliding my arm out of it. I started on the other strap even slower, just to see how long he would last. His eyes burned brighter the longer I took and finally he jumped on the bed, pushed me down, grabbed my bra, and ripped it open.

I opened my mouth to yell at him, but all that came out was a moan. His mouth and hands were on my exposed nipples. He sucked and licked and nibbled, everything almost too rough but not enough at the same time. I was panting beneath him, squirming and reaching.

"I'm clean."

I was still trying to catch my breath as his face hovered over mine.

"I am too, but we've still been using condoms."

"Is that what you want?"

I blinked at him.

"If all I have is one night with you, I want to feel every fucking inch of you. I don't want anything blocking me." His heated words made me shiver, and I nodded.

"I have an IUD, so we don't have to worry about that part of it. But so help me Dory, if I catch an STD from you, I'll cut your dick off."

He grinned. That stupid, cocky smirk that always made me a little weak in the knees. "As if you'd risk damaging this, Amaryllis."

He pushed inside me with one thrust. I gasped, not expecting it, but loving the pain mixed with pleasure that Dorian always seemed to deliver.

"Fuck," he groaned. "You feel even better than I imagined."

"How many times have you imagined this?" I gasped and groaned as he started a steady pace that had him slapping against me every time he thrust forward.

"Too many." He reached up and grabbed a pillow to put under my hips. The elevated position allowed him to hit my g-spot even better as he stayed on his knees and pounded into me. "Every time I hear you screaming and moaning in another room, all I can picture is your beautiful pussy spread out for me, and you calling my name as you come."

The intensity he stared at me with might have scared me but that was before I knew exactly how he felt.

"I feel like I've been walking around with a never ending hard-on the last couple months," he said.

I guess that would explain the extra surly attitude.

"Why didn't you do anything about it?" My words came out between pants.

"You mean like go find a random hookup?"

I nodded my head.

He grabbed my right leg and placed my calf on his shoulder before leaning forward. My eyes rolled into the back of my head at the extra fullness and I whimpered.

"Because I can't get you out of my fucking head, Lyss." His hips kept pumping as he looked down at me with a rawness that I had never seen from him before. "You fill my thoughts with your laughter, your dirty looks, your complete disregard for my status."

"In my defense, I didn't know who you really were when we met."

He smiled and stopped moving his hips. "Would you have acted any differently?"

"Hell no, and don't stop." I propped myself up on my elbows. "You have some big words to live up to tonight. You want to sit and chat instead? Maybe you can braid my hair."

Dorian laughed. He sat back up and pulled out of me. "Roll over."

"I'm not a dog." I glared at him.

He leaned forward so our noses were almost touching. "Then don't act like such a bitch."

I gasped with mock outrage as he laughed. He had never sounded so free, so relaxed before. I pushed at his chest until he fell backwards and I climbed on top of him. I slid onto his cock easily. His hands held onto my hips as I rocked back and forth.

"Who's the bitch now?" I smirked.

"Go ahead and have your fun." Dorian pushed my hips down harder onto him. "Then I'll have mine."

I rode him, rocking and bouncing on him. He reached between us to play with my clit. I gasped his name and my nails scraped down his chest. I was close, so close. Then he pushed me off of him.

I growled like an animal in heat and tried to climb back on him, but he overpowered me until I was face down on the bed. He picked up my hips and shoved into me. I pushed back and soon I was riding that precipice again. He reached around to rub my clit again, and this time, I exploded. I moaned his name into the bed. He pumped a few more times before holding still, pushed into me as far as he could.

I collapsed onto the bed and he fell next to me on his side. After a minute, I got up to go to the bathroom, brushing Dorian aside when he offered to get me a towel.

When I came back out, Dorian stared at me just as hungry as before.

"You already up for round two?" I asked, arching my eyebrow.

He looked down at his semi-hard dick. "Maybe not completely, but that doesn't mean you aren't."

"Let's see how well you keep your promises." I climbed back onto the bed as Dorian got off.

"Lay down and get comfortable, because you're going to be in this position for a while."

"So bossy," I muttered as I obeyed and laid back on a pillow.

Dorian grabbed something from under his mattress. "Hand."

I reached my hand out, and he attached a leather wrist cuff that was attached to a strap. He walked around the bed and repeated the same thing on the other side. My arms were stretched out across the bed, keeping me pinned where I was.

"I always figured Ledger to be into the kinky stuff." I tugged at the strap, testing its strength.

"Ledger wouldn't say no, but he's not as particular as to how he gets it." He reached under the mattress towards the bottom and pulled out more straps to wrap around my ankles.

When he was done, he stood back with a smug grin. I pulled at the straps. I could barely move my arms. My legs had a little more slack, but I couldn't even close them all the way by putting my knees together. I was spread open and on display for him.

"Let's see what you got, Your Highness." I tried to play unimpressed, but I was already growing increasingly wet between my legs.

Dorian turned and went into his closet. When he came back out, he held something in his hand and wore a maniacal smile.

I said nothing, but watched him with a little more worry mixed in with my curiosity.

"I promised you wouldn't be able to scream my name by the time I was done with you. This is to make sure that it happens." He held up his hand and showed the vibrator he was holding. It was a Hitachi, one of the ones you plugged in. I had never used one myself, but I heard they were amazing. In the right hands. I wasn't sure if it would be ecstasy or torture in Dorian's. I tugged a little harder at my restraints.

"How many other girls have you used that on?" I asked.

"None." He plugged it in next to his nightstand. "As I'm sure you saw, I'm perfectly capable of satisfying someone with just my two hands and my dick." He stroked his dick as he stood next to me. "I've never had any reason to add toys to my repertoire. All of this," he gestured to my restraints and the large vibrator he had laid next to me, "is just for you."

I stared at him, surprised. "Are you telling me you planned on this happening?"

Dorian huffed out a laugh and shook his head. "I tried everything to prevent this from happening, but I like to be prepared." He climbed onto the bed and settled between my legs. "After watching you with your little toy, all I could imagine was being in control and having you at my mercy. Now I get to play out my fantasy." He leaned down and bit my inner thigh before soothing it with his tongue. "You have a safe word, Amaryllis?"

I thought for a moment and then smiled. "Marlin."

Dorian rolled his eyes, and I laughed.

"You're going to pay for that, flower." He wrapped his hands around my legs to hold them apart and maintained eye contact with me as he leaned down to lick my clit.

My breath caught. His tongue circled, and I moaned. He continued tonguing me as I laid helpless before him. The feeling of being unable to move helped heighten every touch from Dorian. His hands stroked my stomach, pinched my nipples, squeezed my hips. He pushed me higher and higher and then—

"What? Why'd you stop?" I asked breathlessly. He was still so close I could feel his breath on my pussy as he replied.

"Oh, sorry, were you close?"

I growled. "If you don't know the answer to that, maybe you're not as good as you thought."

"Don't worry, flower. You'll get your finish. You'll get plenty of them." He put his face back into my pussy and started again.

He brought me to the edge again and again and again. By the fifth time, I was begging him to let me come.

"What was that?" He sat up on his knees. His face was wet with my arousal and he made no move to wipe it off.

"Let me come." I tried demanding it, but it came out as a plea.

"I thought we were having fun."

I tried kicking him, but didn't get very far. "If you're not going to finish me, then untie me so I can do it myself."

"You have a safe word. Use it if this is too tough for you."

He knew the exact thing to say to prevent me from using the safe word. I wouldn't back down from a challenge, especially from him.

I narrowed my eyes. "Maybe you just don't know how to close the deal."

He leaned his head back as he laughed. "Nice try, but your barbed words hold no power when I have you pinned down at my mercy."

He put two fingers in me and stroked upwards. I moaned and closed my eyes. Every nerve ending felt intensified from him leaving me on edge for so long. I felt him lean over me as he continued to fuck me slowly with his fingers.

"Besides, I made you a promise. How can I make you stop screaming my name if you haven't screamed it once?" He whispered the words into my ear.

"Dory." It came out as a growl.

His head dipped down and bit my neck, making me yelp.

"It's almost like you don't want to come." Dorian tsked and sat back up, pulling his hand from me.

I whined at the loss and watched as he wrapped his hand around his cock, that was fully erect once again. He stroked it slowly and closed his eyes. When he moaned low in his throat, I started pulling at my restraints again.

"It feels so fucking good having your wetness all over me." He opened his eyes just enough to look at me under his lashes. "You look so cute when you're angry."

I growled again. "Dorian."

His hand paused, still holding his cock. "What was that?"

"Dorian," I repeated, a little louder this time.

A smile lifted the corners of his mouth. "Mmm, I like the sound of that." He slid his fingers over my slit, brushing against my clit before running them over my lips. "Taste how turned on you are for me."

I kept my eyes on his and opened my mouth, allowing him to stick his fingers in. His eyes darkened as I swirled my tongue around them, tasting the bitterness of my arousal and the saltiness of his mixed together.

"That's a good girl."

Fuck, why did hearing that turn me on so much? First Ledger, now Dorian. I would never be able to hear that phrase without dirty thoughts running through my mind again.

"If you're ready to cooperate, so am I." Dorian leaned down until his lips brushed my pussy lips.

I mewled and tried lifting my hips to reach him.

"What do you say?"

"Please." I just wanted the fucking orgasm. I would do almost anything at this point.

"Please what?"

"Please, Dorian. Please lick my pussy until I come all over your face."

He stared at me from between my legs and swallowed audibly. "Fuck, flower. Say that again."

"Dorian, please make me come." I gasped and moaned loudly at the intensity he attacked my clit. He was done playing around, no more slow strokes, no more alternating directions or trying new techniques. He went straight to what I liked most and stayed there. His fingers slipped inside me and started stroking, adding to the delicious sensations. I grabbed at the straps, desperate for something to hold onto as he attacked me.

"Dorian. Yes. Don't stop." I was getting close, and I was terrified he would stop again and leave me hanging. But he didn't. He kept going until I finally reached my climax.

"Fuck! Dorian!"

He kept licking me until I was through every wave of my orgasm. I laid panting as he sat up on his knees with that smug smile men get. I was too worn out to even care, though. He deserved to have that smile.

"Do you know how sexy you sound when you scream my name while you're coming?" he asked.

I chuckled breathlessly.

"Let's see what sounds you make when you can't speak anymore."

He reached over me and grabbed the vibrator. I had completely forgotten about it.

"Don't I get a stretch break or something?" I asked breathlessly.

"You know the magic word. Whenever you're ready to quit, just say it." He pushed a button and a low buzz filled the air.

Damn him. "Fine, bring it on, Dory."

An evil glint was in his eye as he smiled. "I was hoping you'd say that."

He placed the head of the vibrator against my still sensitive clit. I squealed and tried to move, but I couldn't. With his free hand, he held one of my legs to the side, opening me up to him more. Just as I was getting used to the vibrations and start enjoying it, he turned up the intensity. I quickly came again.

"Don't forget to say my name," he reminded me.

"It's too much. Take it off." I moved my hips from side to side as much as I could.

"My name," he said.

"Dorian!" The sensitivity started wearing off as the feeling of another orgasm started building up again. I stopped wiggling and waited. Just as I was about to orgasm again, he turned up the vibrator once more.

I screamed his name as the orgasm ripped through me almost painfully. I tried to close my legs as much as I could, but he moved himself closer so he could keep them open with his own legs. That left his hand free to tweak my nipples and send more sensitivity between my legs.

He kept the vibrator firmly in place. A smile was still on his face as he watched me squirm and pant beneath him. He turned it up a couple more times, and I screamed as I orgasmed two more times in quick succession.

I could barely form words at this point. I couldn't catch my breath. My stomach was sore from clenching so hard each time I came. The buzzing between my legs was a delicious torture that I couldn't decide if I wanted more or less of. After I orgasmed once more, it turned off.

"You still with me, flower?"

I nodded my head, unable to do much else.

"I think I finally rendered you speechless." The smugness in his voice was prominent.

"Fuck you," I whispered, surprised I could even form the words and get them out.

"As you wish." Dorian leaned over me and stuck his dick inside me.

While my clit was sore and practically numb at this point, my vagina sure wasn't. More pleasure shot through me and I gasped.

Dorian moved quickly inside me, each thrust sending me further out of reality. It was too much and not enough. So much pleasure and so much pain. I rode that precipice until he groaned and filled me again.

He slid off me, and I closed my eyes, trying to catch my breath. A damp washcloth pressed against my tender pussy. Dorian unbuckled me from my restraints, rubbing each wrist and ankle as he did so. He finished cleaning me up as I still laid sprawled out before laying down next to me.

He wrapped an arm under me and rolled me on my side, so I curled against him. Perspiration coated his forehead and his hair was messed up, but his jaw wasn't tense. There was no vein on his neck, ready to pop while he looked at me. His eyes weren't narrowed or glaring at me, but closed and relaxed. His mouth wasn't frowning. It was actually smiling. Just barely, but it was there.

"Why are you staring at me like that?" He asked.

"Because you almost seem happy." My voice was still hoarse, so it came out as a whisper.

He laughed softly and turned his head to look at me. "Why does it seem like that bothers you?"

"Because it feels like I might be the one that caused it."

Dorian wrapped an arm around my waist and scooted closer to me. "That might be because you are the one that caused it."

I shook my head. "I don't get it. All we've done for months is fight. I'm in a relationship with three of your best friends. How is this even a thing?"

"Fighting isn't all we've done, Lyss."

I traced the line between his abs. "What else have we done then, Dory?"

He smirked at my nickname for him instead of glaring and turned on his side. His right hand supported his head and his left trailed up and down my back in slow circles and swirls.

"We hang out by the pool all the time."

"That's the group."

"But we were both there."

I pushed his shoulder, so he rolled onto his back and straddled his waist. "Still doesn't count." I smiled down at him as I ran my fingertips slowly down his stomach.

His finger tightened on my thighs as he eyed my breasts. "You know why it can't be like this."

My hands paused from stoking his torso as I sighed deeply. "I know." I looked up and met his eyes. "One night, right?"

"One night," he agreed.

I tried to hide my yawn from him, but he noticed anyway.

"How about we take a quick nap and resume our one night in a couple of hours?"

I nodded and curled into him as he pulled a blanket over us.

Chapter 28

Lyss

Dorian's pillow was cold by the time I woke up in the morning. Our one night was over and I wasn't sure if I was upset or happy to have those memories with me. I dug through his t-shirts and found one I liked because he wasn't getting it back. He had my panties; I was keeping a t-shirt. I opened his door a crack and peeked out, making sure the coast was clear. Even though I knew everyone else knew exactly what we had done last night.

I showered in my room, the hot water soothing my sore body. I chewed on my lip as I got dressed. Would things change between Dorian and me now? Would we go back to pretending to hate each other? Could I pretend to hate him still? We did after the night he watched me get myself off, but it was still different.

"Morning, Lyss." Ledger threw open my door, and it banged on the wall.

I yelped and jumped. "Ledger! You scared the shit out of me."

"I tried to knock, but you didn't answer. Dorian scramble your brains pretty hard last night?" He winked at me.

My cheeks heated, but I didn't deny it.

"I have a few errands to run before we head out tonight. I was wondering if you wanted to tag along."

Ledger always kept my mind occupied, and I hadn't had much alone time with him since he had been back. And it would give me some distance from Dorian, which I really needed right now.

"Yeah, let me just throw my hair up and we can go."

I stared out the window as Ledger drove. I didn't think I'd ever tire of seeing the large variety of foliage and different wildlife around here. All-Star by Smash Mouth came on and Ledger turned up the volume. He grabbed my hand and threaded his fingers through mine. He started singing along with the lyrics, making overly cool, exaggerated facial expressions. I laughed at his antics and joined him in singing.

We sang along with several songs by the time we reached a local diving shop. Ledger resumed our handhold when we got out of the car and we went inside. A little bell jingled, announcing our entrance.

"Ledger, we haven't seen you in for a bit. How's it?" A small man with dark skin and slicked-back hair came out from the back and did the man-hug with Ledger. Ledger grasped the man's hand and leaned in, but didn't fully return the hug, since he refused to let go of my hand.

"Aaron, it's been a minute, man."

"You boys getting ready for another trip?" Aaron looked at me curiously, but kept his focus on Ledger.

"Yeah, and I need to get my girl here some gear." Ledger pulled me a little closer to him and wrapped his arm around my waist.

Aaron's eyebrows shot up. "Your girl, huh?"

"Yup. This little doll here is my Lyss." He leaned down to smack a kiss on the top of my head.

"Hi." I waved awkwardly.

"Nice to meet you, I'm Aaron." He stuck his hand out politely, but Ledger turned me as I reached out to shake it.

I looked up at him, confused. He leaned down to whisper in my ear. "I don't mind sharing you with my brothers, but no other man is going to touch what is mine."

Oh, boy. I wanted to tell him I'd touch whomever I wanted, and that I was my own woman, but my heart just fluttered and sent shocks of desire down my pants.

Thankfully, Aaron seemed to understand what Ledger did with no explanation. Maybe it was more bro code or something. He began showing us around, pointing to different items and explaining about them. When Ledger said I needed some gear, it apparently meant a pole spear, a diving knife, a diving flashlight, and a shark deterrent bracelet. Ledger had me hold several styles of each to see what felt most comfortable in my hands before handing the items we chose to Aaron. He also grabbed a few items that I was sure were for him and the other guys. Different tips for the spears, several knives, and holsters for them.

Aaron rang us up at the register, and we were on our way.

We stopped for burgers and a shake at a little shack by the beach. Ledger wore a hat and glasses to cover his face and threw on a long-sleeved shirt to hide his telltale tattoos. I told Ledger what I wanted, then carried a blanket he kept in the back of his car and set up a spot in the sand. I wrapped my arms loosely around my knees and watched the ocean.

The waves were methodical and soothing as they gently lapped at the shore. Kids squealed and laughed as they splashed in the water. A few people were further out with boogie boards riding the waves towards the shore. There were even a couple of surfers. The waves weren't big enough for a very fun ride, but judging by the shaky legs and the time it took them to get up on the board, they were beginners and these soft waves were perfect for them. Birds called out as they flew overhead.

Ledger plopped down next to me and handed me my caramel cashew shake.

"What's going through your mind, doll?"

I dug through the ice cream until I found a full cashew and scooped it into my mouth. Ledger ate his cherry chocolate chunk shake quietly until I was ready to talk.

"You see pictures of popular beaches and they're packed. Like rows and rows of people jammed together, just to be near the water. Yet, most people don't go any further than twenty feet from the shore."

"Crazy right? Kinda like how most oceanids can't go much further onto land than the beach."

"There's such a small portion where our worlds intersect. Obviously, there are exceptions like you guys."

"And you as of tonight."

I nodded my head. My thumb went to my mouth so I could chew on the nail. Ledger grabbed the offending digit and examined the bitten-down, ragged nail.

"You nervous?" He kept holding my thumb and rubbed his up and down it softly.

I nodded my head. "You guys grew up knowing about humans. I grew up with the Little Mermaid and Jaws as my peek into ocean life. What if the transformation doesn't work? Or whatever magic I have floating through me isn't enough to last long?"

"Doll." He gave my hand a gentle squeeze, and I turned to look at him. "Do you really think we would let anything happen to you?"

"Not on purpose."

"No, we would never let anything happen to you. We would move heaven and hell to protect you." His eyes were intense and all traces of his joking manner were gone. "Even Dorian."

I broke eye contact at that. Suddenly, my milkshake looked very interesting.

"You wanna talk about last night?" Ledger asked.

I laughed, but it came out more like a scoff. "What's there to talk about? I'm sure you know it was only one night. Just a scratch to get it out of our systems."

Ledger's laugh was genuine. "Is that what you really think? You're as stupid as him. Not that you're stupid." He backpedaled when I shot him a dirty look. He took his hat off to brush his hair back and slid the cap back on. "We've talked about how important communication is. You both think that you can forget each other, but knowing the both of you the way I do, last night just made that even more impossible than it was before."

My eyes stung, and I blinked rapidly. "Whether or not last night had happened, nothing can happen with us."

"I know." Ledger's voice was low. He draped an arm around my shoulders and I leaned against him.

A lone tear slipped from the corner of my eye and dripped its way down my cheek. "I have an amazing relationship with you, Rook, and Jem. I shouldn't be upset that the asshole of the group can't be part of it."

"Doesn't make you love him any less."

I sat up and pushed him off me. He fell to the side, catching himself with his elbow.

"Love? Who the hell said anything about love?" He was insane. Love? Dorian? Nope, no, not a chance.

Laughter spilled from his lips as he sat back up. "Lyss, you love him as much as you love us. Something about his sourpuss personality makes your heart beat faster, just like it does around us. Admit, you love us, you love all of us."

"Whoa, buddy, slow down there." I held my hands up facing him.

He got to his knees and launched himself at me. I shrieked as he pushed me down and laid his chest across mine. He held my face in his hands and looked at me with a huge grin.

"Come on, doll, you love us as much as we love you."

"As much as you love me?" I whispered. Did he just say he loved me?

"I am irrevocably in love with you," he said.

"You're quoting *Twilight* again." And I was still trying to comprehend what he was telling me.

Ledger sat up on his knees and straddled my waist.

"There are kids out here." My words said I cared about traumatizing the little crotch goblins, but I didn't try the slightest to wiggle away.

"Amaryllis Bardot, I only use your full name, so you know how serious I am. I am in fucking love with you."

I couldn't even get mad at the full use of my name. I just stared at my reflection in his sunglasses as he grinned down at me. When my shocked face annoyed me enough, I reached up to take off his hat and sunglasses.

"Say that again."

He leaned down until our noses were touching. "I fucking love you. I know all those other bastards do too, but they can tell you themselves. Just remember, I was the first one to tell you."

I giggled and kissed him.

"Now, I don't want you to say anything until you're ready, but do you have anything to say?" He looked at me with a knowing smile.

"I love you." My voice was soft, but it didn't waver. I knew I had been falling in love with these guys, but now I knew I had hit bottom and splattered. My heart was divided between them equally.

"Sorry, I couldn't hear you."

"I love you, Ledger St. James." I was louder this time.

"Damn right you do." He leaned down and kissed me again. His hands framed my face, and I held onto his forearms.

Ledger lifted his head up slightly and turned towards the right.

"Shit, I think we've been recognized."

I turned to where he was looking and saw a group of girls watching us. One of them had her phone pointed towards us like she was filming.

"Come on." Ledger stood up and grabbed my hand. We left the food and blanket on the beach and ran towards his car, laughing the whole way.

He peeled out of the parking spot and headed back towards the house.

In usual Ledger style, he had lifted my spirits and chased away my bad thoughts. For a little bit, at least.

Chapter 29

Lyss

Rook and Jem were in an intense battle when we got home.

"He's right behind you," Rook yelled.

"Which is why I can't see him. Throw a shell at him."

Rook hit a button, and Wario launched a blue shell at Toadette.

"I want to play next round." I sat between the two of them, leaving Ledger to bring in our updated arsenal.

Rook's aim was off and hit Jem's character, Luigi. Toadette passed him and won the game.

"Damn it, Jem." Rook's voice was all growly. "We lost to a pink mushroom."

"At least I was in front of her for most of it."

I climbed into Rook's lap when he really did growl. My knees sat on either side of his hips and I rested my hands on his shoulders.

"Easy there, big guy." I leaned forward and kissed him. "There are much more fun ways to take out your frustrations."

Rook cocked his head and smiled. "What did you have in mind?"

I grinned and rocked my hips.

"I was winning until he hit me. I'm more frustrated." Jem grabbed my arm and pulled me onto his lap, but Rook kept hold of my hips so I was stretched between the two.

I squealed and wiggled when Rook softly bit my exposed hip and Jem licked my neck.

"Which one is it going to be, siren?" Jem asked.

"Do I have to choose?" I stuck out my lower lip.

His gaze softened. "Not if it's going to make you have that look." He leaned down again so he could whisper in my ear. "The only time I want to see your lips sticking out is when I'm pulling my cock from your mouth."

I gasped at Jem's words, and my jaw dropped. He grinned wickedly and winked. My sweet boy had a dirty mouth, and I was loving it.

"Before you guys get all naked and sweaty, someone needs to show Amaryllis how to use a pole spear." Dorian rounded the corner and headed to the table that Ledger was piling stuff on.

I untangled myself from the boys and we followed him to the table.

"Pink? You got her a fucking pink pole spear?" Dorian ran his hand down his face.

"They didn't have turquoise, so we went with the next best thing." I grabbed my pole spear off the table. "Besides, check out this grip." I flipped the pole, so it was pointing up, and all the guys took a large step away from it. "It has this twisty thing to hold on to it better. And some good rubber, so the twisty thing doesn't move." I tried to remember what Aaron had told us about this one.

"It also has a nice pointy thing on the top. Don't forget about that," Dorian added dryly.

"That's right. Want to be my target while I practice, Dory?" I looked over my shoulder at him and for the first time this morning, he met my eyes. Heat pooled low in my stomach. No, it was just one night. One night, you damn horny vagina. His lips quirked up ever so slightly, as if he could tell the inner struggle I was having with myself.

"Thanks for the offer, but I prefer to do the sticking."

And he did an excellent job at it, not that I would admit it to his pompous face. If my screams and the scratch marks on his torso didn't give me away, my words sure as hell wouldn't.

"Rook, will you give her a rundown of the basics so she hopefully doesn't shoot one of us in the ass?" Dorian asked.

"Like you wouldn't want it in the ass," I muttered.

"What was that, Amaryllis?" Dorian looked at me with a raised brow.

"Nothing." I smiled sweetly at him and wrapped my arm around Rook's. "Come on, big guy, show me how to use this thing."

Rook took the spear from my hand and carried it while we walked down to the gym.

"A pole spear is pretty simple. You have the tip, the shaft, the grip, and the band." Rook pointed to each part he named off. "To shoot the spear, you put the band between your thumb and forefinger, pull it tight until you're holding onto the grip. Use your other hand to help aim, holding it loosely. When you're ready to shoot it, release the grip and it'll go."

I watched Rook's demonstration carefully. It looked easy enough. Stretch, hold, aim, release. Rook grabbed a beat-up archery target and set it in the middle of the room.

"Do I get to try now?" I grinned a little maniacally at being able to use the pointy weapon.

Rook looked at me warily. "You seem a little too excited to use it."

I tried to tone down my smile and look a little more nonchalant about it.

Rook stood next to me and handed me the spear. I tried to follow his steps, but my hand kept slipping when I tried stretching the band. Large arms enveloped me as Rook stood behind me. He took my top hand and moved it to just above the grip so it wouldn't slide anymore when I pulled on it. Then he tucked his hand over mine in the band and helped me stretch it until I was grabbing the grip. When I was securely holding it, he let go of the spear and put both hands on my hips.

"Now aim and release."

I focused on the red center and aimed the pole towards it. When I released it, it hit the edge of the target.

"Not bad. Let's try one more time." Rook grabbed the spear and handed it back to me. He helped me set it up again and gave me a couple more tips on how to hold my arms. This time when I shot it, it hit inside the circle. It was the biggest circle, but still. We worked on it several more times. Each time Rook adjusted me or gave me another suggestion. After a few tries, I could load it on my own. Then I was hitting close to the red circle in the center. Even though he didn't need to, Rook kept his hands on my hips, his fingers massaging me lightly.

I began focusing more on his touch and he chuckled when my aim missed the target completely.

"No fair." I put my hands on my hips and pouted. "You're distracting me."

"Remember what Jem said about your pouty mouth?"

"Jem isn't here," I said.

"Doesn't mean I don't agree with his thoughts."

"You want to watch me suck Jem's cock?"

Rook's eyes darkened. I loved getting my gentle giant riled up.

"His, mine, Ledger's, or Dorian's. I don't give a fuck, little guppy." He towered over me as he looked down. "But someone's going to fill that mouth if you keep up the pouting."

Holy mackerel. My mouth went dry, and I stared at Rook hungrily. I licked my lips, then slowly pushed my lower lip out again.

Rook's hand went to his pants. Just as his zipper slid down, Dorian came in.

"She adequate enough to not kill any of us?"

I leaned around Rook to glare at Dorian.

Rook sighed and slid his thumb down my lips. "Later," he growled. He adjusted his pants and turned around. "She's good."

Dorian was leaning against the wall with his arms crossed. He stared at me as his friend walked past him. "Did I just interrupt something again? That's twice in the last hour."

I walked across the room to grab my spear and took my time to answer.

"I wasn't aware I was on a time frame of when I could show affection or to whom."

"Affection." Dorian scratched at his jaw. "Affection is what you feel towards your mother, elderly uncle, or a small child. Pretty sure the chemistry I'm seeing is much more than affection."

"You're right. I guess it would be more lust." I tried to walk by him, but he put an arm over the doorway and glared down at me.

"Aw, don't tell me you're jealous, Dory." I patted his chest. "Last night was good, but like you said," I dropped my smile and any sort of passiveness I was portraying, "it was just one night."

My spear was thrown to the ground, and I was pulled into Dorian's arms quicker than I could blink.

"Don't be like that."

"Be like what?" I pushed at his chest until he let me go.

"You knew it couldn't be anything more."

"Exactly. So stop trying to cock block me just because yours is." I jabbed my finger at his chest.

His hands balled into fists and that vein on his forehead that only seemed to come out around me made an appearance. I wasn't done, though. There was so much built-up emotion regarding him I hadn't been able to process, and after last night, the dam broke free.

"We fucked. You scratched your itch. Now get over it. We're done. You've made that perfectly clear." Tears burned my eyes as I tried once again to walk past him.

"An itch? You think that's what last night was?" Dorian stood in front of me to block me.

"What would you call it?" I looked up at him, blinking furiously.

"One of the best nights of my life."

My hand cracked across his face and he stared down at me in shock.

"Don't you dare." My voice was barely a whisper as I sneered at him.

"What did I do?" His brows furrowed together. "Lyss, I'm being honest."

"Well, don't!" I whirled away from him. There were no other doors out of here, but there were windows.

"You were mad at me when I kept you at arm's length, and now you're mad when I'm trying to open up to you."

I tried pushing the window up, but it wouldn't move. I reached for the lock, but Dorian's hand covered mine. His front pressed against my back. The position reminded me too much of the one we were in last night, in between one of our many sessions, laughing and snuggling together. On our sides, with his arm wrapped around my waist. It was how we had fallen asleep and the position I had still been in when I woke up with him gone in the morning.

"Stop." My voice was weak, the word barely even loud enough for me to hear, but Dorian heard it just fine.

He let go of my hand and took a small step back. I bit my lip to stop it from quivering.

"Lyss." His voice was just as soft as mine, just as heartbroken. It was the only reason I looked at him.

"Dorian, I can't do this. I can't just be friends and act like nothing happened. Go back to hating me and not being able to stand the sight of me."

"I've never hated you, flower. And I only couldn't stand the sight of you because I knew I could never have you." He brushed my hair back from my face and I had to force myself to remain still and not lean into his hand.

I shook my head. "This can't be happening. You have a freaking princess waiting for you. I'm in love with your three best friends."

"Just the three of them?"

I looked up. "Dorian," I pleaded.

"I know they're all in love with you. They have been from day one, but they're not the only ones you've wrapped around that little finger." He stepped closer so he could grab my hand.

A sob escaped me. "This is a mistake. I can't go with you guys. I can't watch—"

A man I love marry someone else.

He gently pulled me towards him until our chests were pressed together. "I'll go back to trading insults with you if that's what you want."

I laughed weakly.

"Or we can meet behind closed doors when everyone else is asleep, and the world is ours alone. I can take time away from Sulamer to come here and stay at the house occasionally. We don't have to say goodbye. We can find a way to make this work."

I leaned my head against his shoulders. It would be so easy to say yes, to be the other woman. I wouldn't be alone when he wasn't there. I still had Jem, Ledger, and Rook. I could have Dorian, too.

He cupped my chin and tilted my head up, hope in his eyes.

Slowly, I shook my head. "I can't do that. I can't be the one that keeps you from your duties and starts your marriage off with lies and betrayal."

"Grace would understand. It's just a power play, a move on the board to strengthen our kingdoms. It's not like she's in love with me." His voice was pleading. His eyes were desperate.

But all I could focus on was the name he said. Grace. The woman taking a piece of my heart had a name.

"Good luck, Dorian." I stood on my tiptoes and kissed the corner of his mouth.

He didn't try to stop me this time as I walked out the door. I was up the stairs when I heard a crash and a loud, "Fuck!"

Chapter 30

Lyss

I waved the boys off when they saw my tear-stained face, telling them I just needed a moment alone. I went to my room and locked the door behind me.

How had I fallen in love with four men? Even more surprising, how had all four of them fallen in love with me and were okay with sharing? I was already losing one, and I wasn't sure if I could bear it.

I groaned and face-planted onto my bed. I was such a selfish bitch. Three other men adored me; why was I pining over the one that I couldn't have? The one I'd known I couldn't have the entire time. If it was another situation, I'd be able to let him go, and move on. Let the wound heal. But Jem was Dorian's cousin, Rook was his bodyguard, and Ledger was his best friend. I would never be able to avoid him. And I sure as hell would not make the guys stay away from him just for my sake.

I was so worried about coming between them and ruining their relationships that I never considered that I would be the one that couldn't hack it. Knowing I couldn't have Dorian and that I would never be free of him, never able to stop wondering "what if?" every time I saw him, I couldn't do that. And I couldn't avoid him when my other three boyfriends were so closely intertwined with him. I couldn't expect them to cut those ties just because of my weakness.

I straightened my spine and headed towards my closet. I caused this mess. And I refused to make their lives miserable just because my damn heart was greedy. I grabbed a duffel bag and my backpack, filling them with clothes, my laptop, and my nightstand goodies. I grabbed the potion and necklace Morgana had given me last minute.

I was in the middle of writing a note, telling them I wasn't fit for this lifestyle and that I was officially quitting as their social media manager when someone knocked at the door.

"Lyss?" It was Jem. My heart pounded like crazy until I remembered the door was locked.

"Yeah, what's up?" I cringed at the pitchiness of my voice.

"We're going to take stuff down to the boat and make sure everything is ready to go. I ordered pizza and it should be here soon. Can you listen out for it? We'll leave after it gets here and eat on the way."

Perfect. It was like the stars were lining up for me and I hated it.

"Yeah, no problem." I squeezed my eyes at the tears that were forming again.

"Thanks, siren."

He left without waiting for my answer. Good thing, because all I could do was collapse to the ground and sob.

I heard them leave out the back door, then waited a couple of minutes to make sure they were gone. I put my backpack on my shoulders and slung the duffel bag over it.

I listened to the house with my door cracked just to make sure no one had stayed behind before running towards the garage. The keys to my Jeep were on a hook next to the other keys. I grabbed them and threw my stuff in the back seat of the Jeep before opening the garage.

My hands were slick on the steering wheel as I waited for the garage door to open up enough for me to get out. As soon as I had clearance, I drove out like the hounds of hell were on my heels. I kept glancing in my rearview and side mirrors, half expecting for one of the guys to come tearing after me.

As I pulled out of the driveway, I passed the pizza delivery car. I went pedal to the metal as soon as I was on the road. Tears blurred my vision, and I wiped them away. This was for the best. They would get over me quickly. I mean, they were royalty in the sea and rock stars on land. They wouldn't miss me for long. Me? I would heal. It might be a wound that was always a little tender, but I would heal.

I knew I couldn't go to the apartment. That's the first place they would check for me. I could get a hotel, I guess. That would eat up my savings quickly, though. How long would I have to stay away for them to forget about me? Technically, I had nothing holding me here. All my work was online. I could pick up another waitressing job almost anywhere if needed. I could send Gia the money for my portion of rent for however long I needed to be gone or until they found a new roommate.

The best place for me to go was home. I used my Jeep's Bluetooth to call my mom.

"Lyss, I was just thinking about you. How are you doing, sweetheart?"

I took a shaky breath. Just hearing my mom's voice comforted me a little bit.

"Lyss, honey, is everything alright?"

I nodded my head before realizing she couldn't see me. "Yeah, I'm fine. I was just wondering if you and Dad would be okay if I came by and visited for a bit?"

"Of course! You know you never have to ask. When should we expect you?"

"Late tonight. Probably around midnight. Don't worry about waiting up."

My mom puffed out a breath. "You know we will be. We never go to bed that early, anyway."

I smiled. No, they usually fell asleep on the couch until about two in the morning, then made their way to bed.

"I'll keep you updated on my trip," I promised her. "Love you."

"Love you too, dear. Be safe."

I ended the call and took a deep breath. I would go home, get my mind back in order, and keep moving forward. I could do this.

My phone rang, and I looked at the caller ID on my dashboard. It was Jem. I hit the end call button on my steering wheel and almost immediately after, Rook's name popped up to notify me he was calling. Another notification told me I had a text from Ledger.

The tears came back, and I wiped my eyes with the back of my hand before I reached for my phone to turn it off. I couldn't talk to any of them right now. If I did, they would convince me to go back and I couldn't do that to them. This was the best choice and I would have to just keep telling myself that, no matter how much my heart split further into two as I drove away from them.

Lyss and her guys will be back in Tempest's Melody.

Be sure to sign up for the newsletter at authordianalong.com for updates.

About the Author

Diana Long grew up in California, but currently resides in Utah with her husband and three kids. When she's not reading or writing, she's spending time with her family or obsessing on her latest adhd hyper fixation.

Sign up for her newsletter at authordianalong.com for updates on upcoming books and appearances.

She loves making new friends on social media. Feel free to message her! You can find her on the below platforms under: @authordianalong

Acknowledgments

Books are like movies where the actor gets all the praise, but it wouldn't have happened without the producer, wardrobe designer, makeup, and, well, you get the picture. This book would not have been possible without so many different moving parts.

I have to start off with my husband, Dillion, and our kids. Without Dillion giving me time away from our little monsters, getting me my own computer, helping keep the house organized, and words of encouragement, there's no way this would have worked out. Our kids for making me feel like a supermom because I'm writing a book even though they're not allowed to look at it until they're at least 18.

Next, my mom and my sister, Laura. My mom would listen to me click-clack at the computer for hours when I was younger coming up with stories about my crushes on our family computer. Laura, for always being my biggest cheerleader. She'll read whatever I write and the twenty different variations I go through to get the story 'just right'. Plus she'll listen to me brainstorm, complain, and help curb my panic attacks.

Then we get to actual book. Asterielly Designs for the gorgeous book cover. They took the crude concept I pieced together and made it into the beauty you see now. LMO Editing for editing it so quickly and wonderfully. My PA Jennifer Webb for all her promoting it and holding my hand through the release process. My beta readers for reading through and offering their feedback on a newbie author.

There are more, of course, that I can't even begin to name all of them. Facebook groups, TikTokers, YouTubers, all with different advice that I smooshed together to make work for me.

Last of all, to my readers. Thank you for joining me on this adventure with Lyss and her guys.